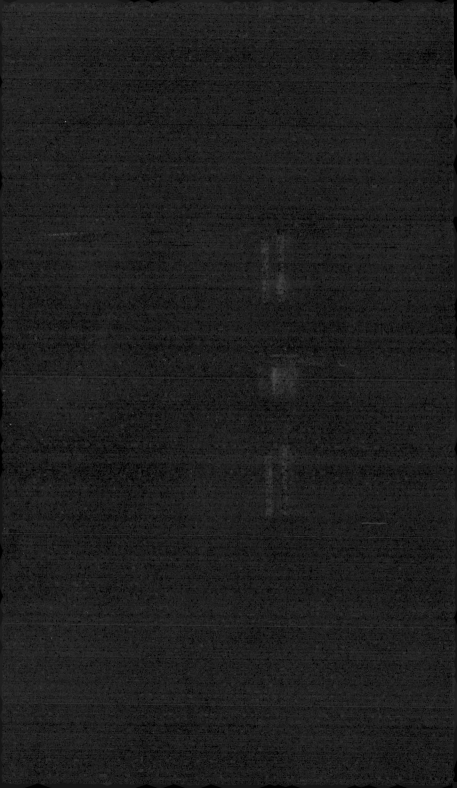

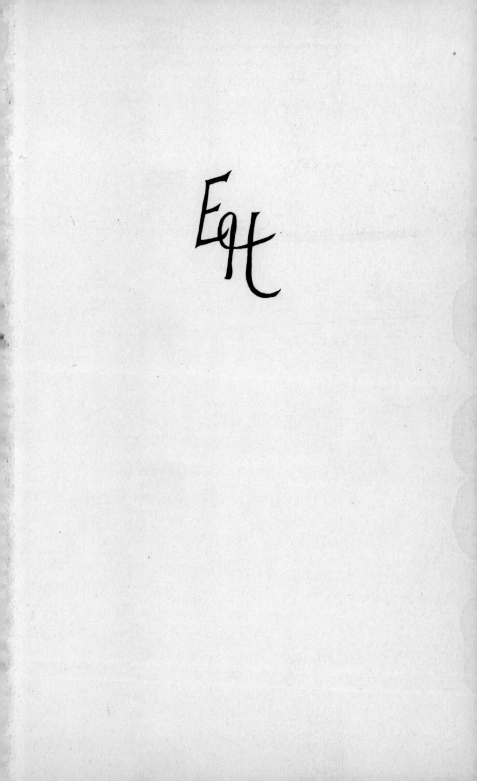

Elizabeth Harrower

A few days in the country and other stories

TEXT PUBLISHING
MELBOURNE AUSTRALIA

textpublishing.com.au
The Text Publishing Company
Swann House
22 William Street
Melbourne Victoria 3000
Australia

First published in 2015 by The Text Publishing Company
Book design and jacket art by W. H. Chong
Typeset in Centaur MT by J & M Typesetting
Printed in Australia by Griffin Press, an Accredited ISO AS/NZS 14001:2004 Environmental Management System printer.

National Library of Australia Cataloguing-in-Publication entry

ISBN: 9781925240566 (hardback)

ISBN: 9781922253330 (ebook)

Creator: Harrower, Elizabeth, 1928– author.

Title: A few days in the country : and other stories / by Elizabeth Harrower.

Dewey Number: A823.3

The publisher gratefully acknowledges the assistance of the National Library of Australia in the preparation of this edition.

A FEW DAYS IN THE COUNTRY
AND OTHER STORIES

Contents

1

The Fun of the Fair

And then, as if the lightning that ripped the sky apart wasn't enough, the lights round the edge of the swimming pool, and even the three big ones sunk into it on cement piles, went out.

At once the solid blackness rang with shrieks and laughter; only Janet was struck dumb to find that she had been obliterated. It was like nothing so much as that astronomical darkness into which she had been plunged last year when they took out her tonsils.

Up to her chin in water, she gave a little squeak of fear and curled her toes into the sandy floor of the pool, entreating them to hang on so that she wouldn't be washed away to the deep end, or out through the pipe that went under the rocks and into the ocean. The Pacific was just over there somewhere. Behind her.

Where was Uncle Hector? She would *call* him.

Except that she wouldn't. He had only brought her tonight because Auntie had given him ten shillings, and because Janet had said 'please' three times, and crossed her heart she wouldn't bother him and Leila.

Then when they met Leila he had said, 'I know. But I had to. Mum's orders. It's for her birthday.'

For a long time—at least ten minutes—Leila said not one word.

Someone close to Janet began to giggle—a slow persistent sound like the pop-pop of an outboard motor. She listened hopefully. Surely no one would laugh like that if anything was wrong?

Just the same, under her breath she said, 'Uncle Hector…' and she licked the salt from her crinkled lips. 'Uncle Hector…'

The surf roared on the beach, and men's voices shouted something about fuses.

The last time Janet had seen Uncle Hector was when it began to rain. He and Leila were in the deep end—in and out of the deep end—practising diving. He called, 'Duck under and keep dry!'

Leila laughed and so did Janet till the stinging of her shoulders made her drift into deeper water and stand with her back covered up, listening to the rain beating against her bathing cap the way it beat on the windows and roof when she was at home in bed. It was almost cosy.

Now, soundlessly and without warning, the lights came on and startled everyone. Janet saw Uncle Hector five yards away. Leila was with him.

'Hello,' she said. 'Where were you?'

'Come on!' Uncle Hector spoke to Janet, but looked at Leila. Leila was nineteen. She had long dark hair, brown skin, and a red-and-white bathing costume.

'Come on!' he said again, swimming away with Leila, making the water foam behind him.

And laughing now, and splashing and looking all round, Janet followed them out.

'I was good, Uncle Hector. You'll tell Auntie I was good?'

Leila was unpinning her hair, wringing out the short skirt of her costume and smiling.

'Huh?' said Uncle Hector.

'In the dark and lightning I was good—you'll tell her?'

'Oh! Yeah! I'll tell her.' He sniffed, pushed back his hair, then stood, hands on hips, feet apart. 'Listen, you two. I'll meet you outside the dressing sheds in five minutes. Five minutes!'

'Bully!' said Leila, pressing her hands against her wet costume. 'You just wait.'

'What for?' He rocked back on his heels.

They stood looking at each other so long then, not seeming to notice that they blocked the path round the pool, that Janet, made reckless by the night, cried, 'For us! You've got to wait for us!'

'Oh, shut up!' said Uncle Hector indifferently.

And Janet did.

She lived with Auntie (who was Hector's mother), and she knew she was a trial. Indeed, she was so far from ideal, in spite of her intentions, that it was suggested in her defence that she'd been born rather badly behaved.

Still, today she was ten. Auntie had talked to her seriously, and said that she must turn over a new leaf and be good and grateful. And she had things to be grateful for…

When he met Janet and his girlfriend, now fully dressed, Uncle Hector said, 'We'll go up there for a while,' and he pointed to a bluff of land where chains of coloured lights— to which were attached chairs and shrieking girls—soared out over the edge of the cliff.

Leila only said, 'Okay,' and swung her red beach bag, but Uncle Hector seemed content.

As they climbed the steps from the swimming pool to the cliff top he remarked, as if he had arranged it, 'It's clearing up.'

Obediently the girls looked, saw the storm clouds, spent, tearing away from the moon, racing out to sea. This had been a day of heat, humidity, and choking dust. Now the air was fresh, still warm, but clear and smelling of the sea.

They reached the top and wandered into the fair. A boy shrieked past on a flying horse, waving an arm at no one in particular. Behind him, wheeling through the night, sat a middle-aged man, neat and sedate in his navy-blue suit. You could see he wasn't on a flying horse for his own pleasure. Perhaps it was to please that girl with blonde curls beside him.

Bemused by the brassy gold, the red and white, the streaming hair and glowing faces, Uncle Hector, Leila and Janet stood with the returning crowds and watched.

The showmen looked at the sky and whistled with relief, stamping on the damp ground. With nasal confidence they cried, 'Roll up, and see the world's greatest spectacle! Fifty years from now you'll be able to tell your grandchildren—'

From every glittering circle a song ground out, and the noisy, discordant medley rose into a night sky lit by the coloured signs of Totting's Fair. Here, where Janet stood, someone was yodelling an old song about an old cowhand…

The bulbs and neon flashed and sparkled, mesmerising the audience, but slowly, and more slowly, the horses flew. They were returning from the daring horizontal to the vertical. It seemed a pity.

Little groups began to drift away. A few people bought tickets from the lady in the red box, but Uncle Hector said, 'We'll see the rest first,' and with Leila clinging to his arm, and Janet following, all eyes, they strolled after the others into the heart of the fair.

Dazzled, badgered and bumped, they wound past the sideshows—the wrestlers, sword swallowers, snake charmers.

A woman said, emerging from the hypnotist's paper cave, 'Yes, I saw him *eat* it, Eck, but how do we know it was a candle?'

Janet longed to hear but, before Eck could speak, she had to go chasing after Uncle Hector, wriggling in and out, looking up to see gleaming teeth bite into hamburgers, faces lost behind drifts of fairy floss. A gang of boys came singing and shouting, arms linked, down the path towards her, and she had to dodge sideways into the Jaws of Death. Uh? She tilted her face up at the name and the picture, and her mouth opened.

Swiftly she dashed out again and came on Uncle Hector almost at once. Leila's violet scent smelled very sweet, and Uncle Hector was looking at her, and laughing in a way that astonished Janet. He seemed so strange, so unlike Uncle Hector! But how lovely it was to see him laugh! And Leila, and all the people! Oh, it was a marvellous birthday night!

'Here, hold these while we go on the Spider. Here's a hamburger to keep you busy.'

Spilling shredded lettuce and tomato sauce over her fingers, the warm roll was stuffed in her hand, and in no time Uncle Hector and Leila were suspended upside down. Janet ate and watched, standing guard over the red beach bag till Leila screamed. Then, till she saw that they were moving down again, she forgot to chew.

'That's my uncle and Leila up there,' she wanted to tell the fat lady next to her. Chewing, she rehearsed it. Then she would say, 'I was ten today. I went for a swim tonight.'

The fat lady turned and walked away with a young man. Disappointed, Janet saw the floral figure recede and vanish in the crowd. She licked her fingers.

'Look at that!' said Uncle Hector, pointing to three short splashes of sauce down the front of her dress.

But Leila said, 'Leave her alone! Pick on someone your own size!'

'Yeah?'

Janet took her damp towel in both hands and scrubbed it ineffectually over her skirt. Undoubtedly Auntie would notice, and she—

They all rode on the Ferris wheel, the razzle-dazzle, and the horses. Then limply Janet waited while the other two threw rubber balls at ducks.

She watched the man behind the counter—arms crossed, striped shirt, bent cigarette—while he watched the balls and the ducks. He was so jolly at first, before they bought the balls.

A paralysing yawn overtook her and she leaned against the side of the booth, but at that moment Uncle Hector flung away down the path and she and Leila had to run after him.

Tossing her long dark hair over her shoulders, Leila winked at Janet and whispered, 'Listen to this!' Then, when they caught him in the space between a tent and a flimsy black building, she said, ranging herself beside Janet, 'Well, no prize, no—' And she jerked her head at the black cardboard building.

Janet read, Tunnel of Love.

Uncle Hector pushed both hands in his pockets and snorted through his nose with exasperation.

'Once Uncle Hector won a prize for his friend Elaine,' she told Leila. 'It was a dog. With spots. Not a real one. Glass.' There was another of those inexplicable silences. Janet added, 'I didn't see it. She told me once.'

Uncle Hector, amazingly, seemed pleased. His grin extended even over her.

Leila snapped, 'Well, what'll we do with *her*?'

'She can look at the giant,' he grinned. 'He's just next door. Here's sixpence, Jan. Get yourself a ticket and go in and see the giant for a while. We'll meet you later. If you're out first, just wait.'

'The *giant*?'

But they had disappeared inside the doorway of the Tunnel. She felt deserted. A *giant*, she thought.

'Hurry! Hurry! Hurry!' cried a man in a brown checked suit. 'The show is about to begin. The greatest romance since Romeo and Juliet. Step up and buy your tickets now! See the greatest giant in the world and his lovely little bride.'

He'd said it. Giant. This was where she was supposed to go, all right. Vaguely, Janet shifted her towel to her other arm, and rubbed the cold patch it had made on her dress. Clutching a ticket she gazed at the man. He said, 'Hurry up, there! In you go!'

She swallowed. 'Yes, but is he? Is he?'

'He's lovely, dear. Hurry! Hurry! The show—'

It was a small tent. About a quarter of its length was cut off by a curtain behind which, presumably, dwelt the giant and his bride. Overhead hung a battery of bare electric light globes.

In front of a low platform, nine or ten people stood waiting, talking in whispers. As if from a great distance they could hear the raucous cries to which they had recently contributed, the mechanical music. But now, by virtue of their dark-green tickets, they were set not only apart from but subtly above the crowd.

Janet drooped with weariness. There was nothing to see—a wooden pole, two wooden chairs—but she looked for a moment or so, and then yawned and buried her face in her towel. Jack and the Beanstalk. Jack the Giant-killer, she thought.

When she opened her eyes she saw on the platform, close to her, straight in front of her, a very small woman. She was much smaller than Janet, but not so young, oh, not young at all. Under the pink make-up, the little face was hard and wrinkled.

On a level, their eyes met, and Janet went cold, then colder, transfixed by the look and by a sudden strange sensation in her chest. The dwarf had never seen her before. The dwarf did not like her.

The dwarf bride smiled at her and Janet shivered. She hugged her towel and bit a piece of the fringe. She stared down at the ground, at her dusty toes poking out of her sandals. To prove that she could, she made them wriggle. When she lifted her head, the little woman was gazing into space, blankly, looking bored, so bored...

Humbly, Janet moved her eyes from the small monkey face to the long, never-ending red-trousered legs that stood beside her. She followed them up. There was a navy-blue coat in the distance, above that a face, above that a red cap.

The face, apart from its distance from the ground, was supremely ordinary—pale, but ordinary. And this was the giant!

Like the woman, he stared without expression straight ahead. There was, from him, no look for Janet, no smile that was not a smile.

As they were meant to do, the audience watched them: no one spoke. But from the back of the tent into the silence came a snicker. Janet felt her arms go hot, and her shoulders and ears. She *wished* Uncle Hector hadn't sent her here.

The giant and the dwarf moved closer together. Then, with a simultaneous craning of necks, they exchanged their first public acknowledgment of each other's presence, a look that was empty yet completely familiar. With an almost audible 'One, two, three...' they started.

'The story of our love begins far away under the blue skies of Africa, where we met and fell in love...'

The giant went on alone, 'I, a tall and shy young man, scarcely dared ask for the hand of the dainty young maiden...'

When he had finished, the dwarf cleared her throat to take up the recital, and, shamefaced, the audience listened.

All Janet knew was that they didn't mean it. They didn't mean a word they said. She blinked at them.

And they don't care if we know it, she thought. They're saying all this and hating us. Love, they're saying.

'Little lady,' the giant repeated. 'Would you mind telling us your age?' He was looking straight at Janet.

'Me?' she whispered.

'Tell him, dear,' said a woman behind her.

She glanced over her shoulder. 'Ten,' she said, and the giant heard.

'A very nice age to be!' he exclaimed. 'Now, if you would step up onto the platform for a moment, all these ladies and gentlemen could see how tiny and dainty my bride appears beside a little lady of ten.'

Janet stared at him. She tried to grow into the ground. Someone gave her a gentle push and she resisted. But the giant reached down with his long, long arms and said, 'Up here. That's the way!' and she was on the stage.

The giant was talking to the audience. He made her take the hand of the dwarf. He made them stand together while he measured the difference in height with a ruler produced from his pocket.

Mechanically, Janet obeyed him. She held the small horny hand. She turned around and felt the small warm back against her own, and the ruler on her head.

'You can turn round again,' the giant said. 'No, this way—so they can see you.'

There was a slight ungentle tug on her arm and she turned to receive from the silent dwarf, so close to her, another long professional smile. The dwarf did not like anyone.

Janet fell back a step and bumped into the giant. He said, 'Well, now, may we both shake you by the hand, and wish you the very best of luck? We'd like you to accept our hearty thanks for your kindness in assisting at this demonstration for the benefit of our patrons.'

The giant bowed and shook her hand. Janet said, 'How do you do?'

And then her hand closed like a giant's over the toy hand of the dwarf. Tremulously she looked down into the hazel eyes. What was it they said to her? Nothing nice. Nothing good.

'How do you do?' said Janet. 'Thank you. Good night.'

The audience clapped. She was on the ground again. The people began to file out of the tent, murmuring self-consciously. A backward glance showed the giant and his bride sitting on the chairs, smoking, looking at the roof of the tent, not talking, and oh so bored, so bored…

Janet looked at her hand.

Outside, it was very dark after the barrage of lights over the stage. Uncle Hector and Leila walked slowly up to the entrance as she came out. They seemed surprised to see her.

Uncle Hector said, 'You got your money's worth, all right.' He and Leila had been through the Tunnel of Love twice.

Mute, Janet looked at their shadowy faces. She held her hand out, away from her. All at once, she was overwhelmed with heavy tearing sobs. She stood isolated in the night, sobbing uncontrollably.

Leila let out a groan, glanced at Uncle Hector and said to Janet, 'What's the matter, Jan? Did the giant frighten you?'

They stood at the entrance of the tent, where the man in the checked suit was preparing to enlist the last audience of the night. He caught the sense of Leila's words and scowled down at her.

'Come over here,' said Uncle Hector, and they wandered away along the emptying paths between the booths, Leila leading Janet by the hand.

Reluctantly Leila stopped again. 'Did the giant frighten you? Was he awful or something?'

Janet shook her head, nodded, shook it again, and wept with such bitter abandon that the two in charge of her began to worry.

'This is lovely!' said Uncle Hector, biting his nails. 'What'll we do?'

'She's *your* relation!'

Uncle Hector, regarding his relation, jerked forward. 'Here! What's the matter with your hand? What've you done to it?

When he understood that it had been shaken by the giant he looked at it with a flattered half-smile, and forgot it.

'What'll we do with her?' Leila said.

Janet sobbed, 'I want to go home! I want to go home!'

'I wish to heaven she *could*,' Leila said. 'Couldn't we put her on a bus?'

While they stared at each other and wondered, Janet drew a little away from them. Amazed, she looked at the sky, and the fair, and her uncle and Leila. She looked at the people who passed. Roughly she wiped her eyes and took a backward step.

'No, I *don't* want to go home,' she whispered.

She moved further down the path.

More loudly she said, 'No, I *don't* want to go home.'

'Where's she gone?' said Uncle Hector, screwing up his eyes in the darkness.

He saw her and started after her but was slowed, then stopped altogether, by the peculiar menace of her expression and the unexpectedness of her retreat. He couldn't imagine what she was up to.

'I'm not coming!' she screamed at him. 'You can't make me. I won't. I'll never go back to you and Auntie.'

She ran a few steps and turned. 'I don't love any of you. I'll never go back.' Aimlessly, frantically, turning and twisting round caravans and tents, up and down the paths of trodden earth, pushing through the thinning crowds, she ran, not crying now, but brilliant-eyed.

2
Alice

She was a little girl with red-gold sausage curls, curls darker than red-gold. She did have this lovely hair. She also had thick creamy skin and grey-blue eyes that wondered. Very young, she read all the stories in which the fairies and the kindest mothers and fathers and the strangers in the woods who were benevolent to lost children said, if not in so many words, 'It is good to be good.' But, even without the painted finger of the fables pointing in that direction, Alice would have been inclined to be good. Babies arrive with dispositions, and this was hers.

Her mother was Scottish born and bred—irrational, raucous, bony, quick-tempered, and noisy. She had no feelings. She was bright, like anything burning: a match, a firecracker, a tree. Alice was as watchful as a small herbivorous animal.

Mother and child were unsatisfied. They looked at each other.

Luckily for the mother, she also had two sons, younger than the girl—golden, milky boys, not made entirely of wood and flames like their mother, nor of guileless life like their sister, but a mixture of both, and somehow not quite enough of either. They were extremely pretty children just the same. Like Alice, the brothers had remarkable hair and eyes, but their great triumph over her was that they were boys. She began to perceive that this, more than curls or thoughtful ways, was what pleased. The question was: could one terribly good girl ever, in her mother's eyes, equal one boy? And the answer was no.

Alice was a feminine, old-fashioned girl. She neither looked like, felt like, behaved like nor wanted to be like a boy. But she did want her mother to notice her, to be pleased with her, to affirm to everyone, 'Alice is here.'

The family had come to Australia from the Old Country, bringing old ways. Alice was, for the century or so of her childhood, a nursemaid, nanny, and servant to her brothers. Knowing the weight the boys bore in her mother's mind, she was aged by the responsibility before she was ten years old. If they ran and fell over, dirtied their clothing, cried experimentally or out of bad humour, if they broke any household idols, or in any way irritated their mother, it was all, all Alice's fault. The child began to have doubts.

Sometimes, when Alice was walking down the street, one passerby would say to another, 'Did you see that gorgeous hair?

What a colour!' And she'd wish dreadfully that her mother had been there. The amazing thing, though, was that if her mother *was* there she never heard it. Or if she did hear she didn't understand. Or if she did understand she didn't care. Visitors learned to praise the boys, and not Alice. Even visitors liked to please her mother. It was safer.

Oh, the family had a father. But he went away to be a soldier and was gone for years. When he came back, he was even more silent than before, and the mother indicated that he was of no account. He went to his mysterious work, and spent almost as much time there as he had at the war. When he returned to the house, it was only to eat and sleep. Much later, after the children were all grown up, he died. The day after the funeral, no one could remember his voice.

Meanwhile, the boys swam in attention and praise, and at an early age had had so much that they never needed it again, could afford to discard that particular life buoy and plunge out with a glossy confidence in their qualities. Alice never even learned to dog-paddle. Who would notice if she sank? The deep end was too risky for a girl whose brilliant dark-red curls could be so easily overlooked.

Now and then a teacher or an acquaintance would toss her a few friendly words. Naturally, if she hadn't needed them so badly, she could have collected ten times as many. But she had never heard of supply and demand, wasn't aware of such a thing as a seller's market, and wouldn't have applied it to her own case if she had. Like a solitary bowerbird, she hid these tiny pieces of blue glass around her nest and treasured them, though frequent inspection soon took their colour away. Alice knew only that something was not fair. Here she was—a good girl, a nice girl, pretty to look at, obedient, kind, clever at school, and with beautiful hair—yet none of it was *good enough*. While the boys were somehow perfect. And not because they didn't try but because they never had to. They were welcome when they arrived.

Because Alice's deepest attention, you might even say her soul, was busy looking back, over its shoulder, she had few acquaintances and no friends. For many years her duties toward the boys, and her strivings to please her mother, took up her whole life. And all this time the mother stayed about the same age; the boys were permanently young, since that was their mother's desire. Only Alice and her father grew old.

One of the boys played the mouth organ and went shooting; the other sketched and painted, and in the interest of his muscles trained at the local gymnasium with a group of amateur boxers. There were photographs of him, gloves raised, head lowered, forehead threateningly wrinkled. There were photographs of football teams in which both boys were illuminated, among all the other hefty thighs and striped jumpers, by their saintly blond heads. On Saturdays and Sundays, they went surfing at the local beaches, taking their girlfriends.

Alice had none of these occupations. She would have

liked to take piano lessons, but these were the Depression years, whatever that meant. It was the Depression that made everyone unhappy. Quite possibly her mother might have valued her greatly if it weren't for that. Who knows? (Yet her mother was not unhappy, being herself.) Alice baked little cakes for the boys' picnics, as her mother told her to. Though she never complained, she did feel resentful, baking in the summer heat. Temperatures outside in the shade went over the hundred mark; the heat in the kitchen, with the oven on, was not investigated. Alice fainted sometimes.

The house was always busy with people—'that little Robinson woman' or 'that little Fenwick man'—coming to see her mother. They sat upright on the big leather sofa or on the edge of one of the chairs, while her mother marched to and fro hypnotising them with her enormous effrontery, her energy, her noisy laughter. If the visitors wanted advice of any description, she never hesitated. She was the most positive person any of them had ever come across. Though her opinions were based on nothing but inspiration, and were wrong as often as the law of averages allows, she had the virtue of being certain of everything in uncertain times. The relief of it! The little men and women went away livelier, diverted from their troubles, forgetting to sigh for whole blocks as they walked home through the flat suburban streets. (Only the stars were wonderful in that place, but because they were always there they were never noticed.)

Alice's mother told her little men and women about the Old Country. She told them about snow. They had never seen snow, but they were willing to try to picture it. With incredulous half-smiles, they listened to her account of the stuff—so pure, so clean, so cold, the very opposite of everything here. Did it exist? Was there really an Old Country? Their eyes were wistful. They knew it was true. It was just that they couldn't quite believe it.

If the father came in while they were there, he walked straight through the room without a word or a look. Everyone was used to this and thought nothing of it. The mother's vehement talk, her triumphant shouts of laughter, continued without interruption.

No one in that town could have ambitions beyond not being hungry, not being in debt, not being unemployed. Later in life, Alice never found anyone who shared her impressions of her youth and that time. Either she moved in different circles from those she had known then or the others more easily forgot. She remembered everything: crowds of men going nowhere in army-surplus sandshoes and khaki overcoats, men with swags of dead rabbits for sale, men with small suitcases full of useless items (no more than an excuse to talk), like those small bottles of startling green and red dye that her mother bought. For years, they stood in the pantry. No one knew what they were supposed to be for. Years later still, some of the boys' children found and drank them, watered down, as a test of courage. They didn't die.

Head bent, polishing the boys' shoes or occupied with some other mother-pleasing chore, Alice listened to the travelling men, knowing only that they absolutely could not be turned away. It was her mother's nature to give; she was expansive and generous, though her tongue must often have poisoned the food she distributed so willingly at the back door. No charge could be laid against Alice's mother. She was only herself. The men's pride? Alice's feelings? A good dose of castor oil was what they all needed.

Alice had a little job somewhere. Thin, pale, she ate a banana in the midday heat, thinking of the Old Country and the clean cold. The buildings *there* had stood for generations. *Here* was an enormous expanse on the map but a small black hot place in reality. Four flat black miles in a tram to the coast, through weeds and tumbledown one- and two-storey buildings. The people, her mother often said contemptuously, were like Gypsies. But they were not imaginative or gay, as Alice thought Gypsies might be, only temporary-seeming, accidental, huddling about the masses of steelworks and hotel bars.

And Alice in the midst of this. If her mother could not like her or notice her ever, how terrible! How terrible! Sometimes people made the opening gestures of friendship in the rough style of the district, but often Alice missed them entirely, as a tired person might, for was her mother not holding the floor, making speeches about 'my sons, my boys'?

At other times, Alice treasured any overture.

'Mr Wade said to me…'

'Sally Grey wants me to go…'

No one heard. If she persisted until her mother was forced to listen, her mother's eyes went blank. Or she was actually listening to the races on the radio three rooms away. Or she would talk Alice down with instructions and demands. Because her mother was her mother, and there was no one else, Alice thought she was marvellous.

One day, Alice said, 'Eric Lane wants to take me to—'

For the first time, her mother attended, standing still.

Eric was brought to the house, and Eric and Alice were married before there was time to say 'knife'. How did it happen? She tried to trace it back. She was watching her mother performing for Eric, and then (she always paused here in her mind), somehow, she woke up married and in another house.

Eric was all right, but he was almost as young as she was and knew no more about the world. In fact, he knew less, because this was his birthplace. He had no snowy memories, no castles, no wild cherry trees, no sound stone houses with polished brass and roaring fires, no Halloween, no ghosts or witches, no legends of his own going back to the morning of the world, no proper accent, like the people *there*. At home. Poor Eric had only this empty place where no one belonged, and the Depression, and swimming in the sea with sharks, and sinking and drowning because who would notice *here?* He liked her hair—but still her mother didn't care.

So Alice was with Eric, being a wife. Since Eric was an ordinary boy, and she had these extraordinary memories and her extraordinary mother, Alice was sometimes lively and high-handed with him. He told her that girls with her hair colour had quick tempers. Alice found a sparky temper. For short periods, she planned a flower garden, or worried about her cooking, or sang. But there was no money, except to pay the rent and buy food. There were no books. There was no person to talk to who understood anything more of the world than she and Eric did. There were only rumours, legends about it. The world sounded like such a strange place. They felt shy.

'We were closer to the Middle Ages than to people now,' she said, years later. But that was not it. In those days, only someone like Julius Caesar could have been compared with her mother.

After two or three years, Eric's work took him into the country, where there was no accommodation for wives. And Alice's mother said that she hoped he didn't think any girl of hers was going to rough it in the Australian bush because he was too lazy to get work in town. Gosh! Gosh! Speaking up for Alice! But Eric didn't hold it against her. He thought she was a card, Alice's mother.

Anxious and eager, Alice hovered about her mother's house, still helping with the boys, listening with an inward drooping to endless tales of their exploits. Yet again, she heard about their winning looks; how one of them was known locally as Smiler; how the mother had bought them these expensive garments, that extravagant gadget; how they set about acquiring what they wanted from her—flattering, teasing, kissing, asking, cuddling, demanding, making her laugh.

Alice learned to laugh, too, bitterly. If she said what she thought, her mother's retorts could leave her bleeding, and frequently did. Yet, as soon as the scars had healed, she protested again. Her mother took it that Alice begrudged the boys whatever item they had most recently conjured out of her, and would argue about a piano, or a type of car, till Alice was ready to die. She couldn't say, 'We are not talking about pianos or cars!' because she didn't know this. Something about her mother's argument was murdering her. Ever afterward, she looked at the boys' piano and car with loathing.

From the bush, Eric sent home his money. When he had leave, he came back for a few days. A fair amount of time passed. Then the news all came out in an anonymous letter. Eric had sung a love song to a pretty girl's accompaniment. Eric had slept with the girl. The girl's father was very angry. Alice's mother was very angry. There were meetings and consultations, wild words and tears.

Finally, Alice and Eric moved away from the hideous place with the smoky skies, that hopeless place whose own inhabitants could find no good word to say for it. Now Alice was hours by train from her mother, and there was no money for journeys. Eric was chastened and listless from his joust with experience. Yes, he had sung that love song to the girl in the bush, but he had also shared Alice's snow and, in a way, owned Alice's spectacular hair. It would be nice if she would forgive him, now that they were together. They might go to a dance. He would sing songs to her, too, better songs. He appreciated her cooking. There was some indefinable thing about Alice that he liked so much. She was deep. He didn't understand her. For all these reasons, but particularly for the last, he was willing to love her forever. Oh, Alice!

Eric. He was only a familiar foreigner who looked at her expectantly. She needed to be dazzled.

He was impressed by the strength of her mysterious longings, but he was a follower, too, and two followers together are bound to lose the way. At first, he tried to walk behind Alice, assuming that she knew where they were going. How could he know that she was only trailing her mother, since there was no other leader whose approbation could mean so much? After a while, he began to feel stumped. In his dreams, they wandered hand in hand, but he was no comfort to Alice. She was always looking into the distance, farther than he could see. He was grateful to wake up. Everything was all right, really; it was just that there was a sensation in their small wooden house that, somewhere close by, someone was dying of starvation.

Now that miles of trees and railway lines divided Alice and her mother, a new element entered the world: Alice's talent for remaking reality. Her mother—what a martyr to those wicked boys, that silent husband! How free and easy with the neighbours! Anyone could turn to her. And how the boys and their wives took advantage of her good nature! Alice fumed, pale and silent.

Eric asked if she felt okay. He was rough. The way he arranged his words, awkwardly, with a natural impatience, even when cheerful, would have left marks on Alice if she had cared. Now, when he thought to compliment her in some backhanded way, she looked at him as if he hadn't spoken. As if anything *he* could say... As if *his* opinion... With no feelings even as strong as sadness or contempt, she overlooked his well-meaning efforts to encourage her. He had no idea. Nobody knew. She didn't even know herself.

It dawned on Eric that Alice had something on her mind a great deal of the time. For all he knew, having something on your mind was natural to women. In other ways, she was a good wife. He liked her hair. He even liked her temper. Once, they had had some fun. Of course, they were getting older, two or three years older. But no one had ever warned him that age could subdue you so fast, so soon.

'The boys are all right. Don't worry about your mother. She's okay. She wants to give things to them—let her!' Secretly, he was grieved and envious not to receive a share of any bounty that was on offer. But he wore a sturdy front.

'They impose. They're imposing on her. I can stand anything but imposition,' Alice would say, damped down.

Letters poured out of her, smoking, in terms she would have been afraid to use face to face with her mother. She called her loving names. She called herself her mother's loving daughter. She advised her mother not to give in to the boys' demands. They were mean and nasty. They were insatiable. She hated them (though she didn't say that).

The letters she received in return were slow to come, short, predictable. Still her hopes lifted daily: a letter would arrive from her mother that would mend her life. If Alice had a fault, dangerous to her survival, it was that she was inordinately reluctant to learn from experience. She would not. Because the lesson would be so sad. And she had spent so much of her life going in the opposite direction from the lesson. And still the lesson pursued her, like a monster through the forest. Of course, it was a hard lesson that not everyone has to learn.

The mother visited from time to time. She and Eric jollied each other along. Alice planned for weeks beforehand— everything had to be perfect. Then she could do nothing right. Her ways were different from her mother's, and therefore to be scorned. Sharp laughter, sharper comments, news of the boys rapped out with some exultation. Alice suffered. Her mother laughed. Eric wondered what was going on, and tried a few wisecracks. Then, 'It'll all blow over,' he would say to one or the other. 'She's probably under the weather. Happens in the best of families. Bit of a flare-up, then it's all over.'

No one took any notice of Eric. He was like a gnat, talking his own language to two large creatures who were enemies, but enemies concerned with each other as they were not with him.

Even yet there were days when Alice's looks and ways were pleasing to others. And she would cling to the gift of their willingness to approve of her. All she would allow herself to think was: I wish there were someone I could tell. Not mentioning any names. Artlessly, she marvelled that people thought they could reach her. They were so separate from her. Why couldn't they understand this?

Years went by. The road where Alice had stopped now stretched far in either direction. She didn't want to follow it. Occasionally, she looked along its length. She stood there with a little crowd of girls and women, all with ravishing red-gold curls. There had been this accident, so long ago that none of them could remember quite what it was. A horrible accident. They couldn't get over it. And, unluckily, no one had ever passed by who understood this, or explained that you could walk away, sometimes, from bad accidents.

Once again, Eric's work took him into the country. He didn't want to go, but he had no choice. While he was there, he slept with another girl, and this time there was a divorce. It didn't really matter, though, because the mother had found another man for Alice, a man who might make more money. He was much older than she was, and very different from Eric—demanding, critical, sarcastic, powerful, brutal. He was like Alice's mother in strength, except that he never laughed. Next to him, Alice's mother seemed better.

Now Alice's life was truly hard. No one would have believed how hard it was, but, anyway, no one knew. Now there were two who could never be pleased, two who believed that anything could be bought. This did not prevent her, Alice being Alice, from restoring their images nightly with fresh paint and plaster and rearranging their robes in ever more becoming folds.

The dreadful boys went from bad to worse, persecuting her wonderful mother. The man had a lot to put up with, too, with the world not appreciating him as it should. But occasionally Alice still ventured to wish, when a stranger put a field flower in her hand, that there were someone she could tell.

Nothing changed. Neither the mother nor the man nor Alice. The boys deteriorated slightly, receiving one shock after another, when the rest of the population proved less indulgent than their mother. Everyone grew much older. They had all worked hard.

One of the strangers who sometimes talked to Alice now was a girl, a neighbour. Alice's hair was grey. The girl had no mother or father. For five minutes at a time, Alice would listen to stories of the girl's life, and each thought of small helpful things to do for the other. When the man was ill, as he often was now, being quite old, the girl took the trouble to fetch and carry for Alice. Alice returned the goodwill in more than equal measure: she would never be in someone's debt.

Just the same, this activity was no more pleasing to her than the chirp of a small canary. It was pitiful, in its way, because the girl thought, as had others in the past, that she was really talking to Alice, was friendly with Alice. She didn't realise that Alice had received no sanction for any such behaviour from her mother or from the man. What a strange little girl to think that she mattered, when Alice's mother was frail and ill, and the boys were bleeding her of every penny, and she still thought them ideal in their greed and insincerity.

One day, the girl told Alice that she was soon to be married. Alice was dubious about boys, but she met this one and liked him—a country boy with honest eyes. Regularly now, she heard about the wedding. She always listened seriously, and gave excellent advice, much wiser on the girl's behalf than she could ever be on her own. She was invited to the ceremony and the reception, and would have been mildly pleased to go, but the man was ill. Everything was complicated, as it had always been.

On the wedding day, Alice brushed her hair and looked in the mirror at her sleepless eyes. The latest letters from her mother had complained about Alice and the man in violent terms. They sent presents when she wanted cash to pass on to the ever-hungry boys. Was this complaint fair? Attending to the house and the man, who was ill in bed, drugged, Alice sometimes noticed the clock and remembered what day it was.

At last, the man fed and sleeping again, Alice sat down alone. And then, from the top of the garden path, someone was calling her name, and through the greenery and the late-summer flowers the girl came in her wedding dress and shimmering veil, like a bird or an angel, on her way to the church.

Wonder almost lifted Alice off the ground. Stopping cars, leaving bridesmaids hovering by the gate, the girl floated down. She had thought of Alice, wanted Alice's blessing at this aston-ishing moment. Everything shone with light—the sky, the garden, the girl in white, and Alice. This was like nothing that had ever happened before. The girl and Alice smiled.

Even after the girl left, in clouds and drifts of white, nothing seemed substantial. A buoyancy, an airiness, something quite amazing surrounded Alice. She had no idea what it was called.

Oh, but she wished, she *wished* that there were someone she could tell. Then, in the middle of this tremendous wish, Alice paused: a great thing was beginning to happen to her. A new thought appeared in her mind, yet Alice recognised it as if it had always been there. The thought said, But *I* know. *I* know.

After this she looked the same, and her circumstances didn't alter, but she was a different person altogether.

3
The City at Night

The two tall girls walked along the busy Sydney street: the fair one, Leonie, with superb natural grace, looking neither to right nor left; the dark-haired girl, Janie, self-consciously in her first pair of high-heeled shoes. She turned now and then, when speaking, to look at Leonie, but Leonie's head never turned. The straightness of her gaze, the elegance of her bearing, seemed almost unnatural to Janie.

Janie was sixteen and a half, and had been at work in an office for exactly one day. This evening, saying 'miracle of miracles', instead of going straight home to tell her mother of the intricacies of the switchboard and tea-making, she was going out with beautiful Leonie, sophisticated and seventeen-and-a-quarter and well-made-up Leonie. It was Janie's coming out into Sydney nightlife; it was her growing up.

This is the first time I've walked through the main streets at night, she thought.

'I never knew the city had so many lights,' she said to Leonie, who smiled.

They passed an air-conditioned cinema, and the coolness cut a swathe through the soft night. The strong sweet perfume of frangipani blossoms was fanned through a florist's doorway and hung suspended, a subtle advertisement.

Janie sniffed appreciatively. She caught the tang of fresh-ground coffee, too, and felt hungry.

'We're nearly there,' Leonie said in the round drawling accent she had acquired since leaving school, the shield for her self-consciousness.

'That's good,' Janie breathed, dazzled by the brightness and the crowds of young people who looked as if they knew where they were going, and what they would do when they arrived; dazzled by their clothes, and doubtful for the first time about her new blue dress.

Sophistication and assurance everywhere: it was a relief to be inside at last, at a table for two with Leonie, and the waitress ready with her pad, gazing at herself in the mirror while they studied the menu. Until they had decided on grills and sundaes, and the waitress left, their manner was cold, serious, blasé.

Then they were alone, exposed, the eyes of the other

unavoidable and uncomfortably close across the small table.

Leonie's hands were smooth and creamy, the nails long and polished. She broke her roll and buttered a piece. Janie looked in her bag for a handkerchief, and blew her nose, although it didn't need it.

'I think it's...'

'How did you...'

They laughed awkwardly and pressed one another to speak first.

'I was just going to ask if you'd enjoyed your first day,' Leonie said at last.

'Well, it was all so new...' Janie's voice trailed off; remembering that she had met Leonie in the office, she added, 'But I think I'll like it very much.'

'I hate it,' Leonie said calmly. 'The other girls don't like me and I don't like them. Did you see that today?'

Her straightforward manner made Janie feel abashed and enchanted and partisan.

'Yes, I thought something was wrong,' she said.

She had mentally declared herself on Leonie's side even before her incredible invitation to go out after work: partly because the odds were three against one, partly because the other girls had frizzy hair and ingratiating manners.

Janie stared unseeingly at her plate, where a chop, a ring of pineapple, green peas, and Saratoga chips waited, while her intuition brought forth a judgment. 'It's just that you're different,' she said, forgetting to feel embarrassed. 'That's why it's like that at work.'

She was about to go on when Leonie cut in. 'They told you I am Lithuanian?'

'Yes, but that isn't what I mean.'

Her untrained mind struggled to define the difference she had felt. It was something more subtle, more elusive than Leonie's attractiveness, her cultivated accent, her foreign birth; something more fundamental.

Leonie was pleased and interested. 'What *do* you mean?'

Janie floundered. 'I don't know,' she said helplessly, 'but I know I'm right.'

'Are you different, too?' Leonie asked without malice.

'Yes, I suppose I am,' she said, picking up her knife and fork.

'That makes two of us then,' Leonie smiled, a wide unsophisticated smile, showing even white teeth.

Janie smiled back and felt immensely happy. Leonie was so friendly. She seemed really to like her. She must, or she wouldn't have asked her to come out. And, now that they were out, she was nicer than ever.

Leonie buttered another piece of roll, and asked, 'Have you always lived in Sydney?'

The biographical question had come; the first step in the ritual of making a friendship, as when children say, half boldly, half shyly, 'What's *your* name? Where's *your* house?

What school do *you* go to?'

'No,' Janie said. 'I came from the country when I was thirteen. We've been living in Manly ever since. When did you come here?' she asked, interested in Leonie's foreign background, but doubtful about mentioning it. She wondered how it must feel to be foreign.

'When I was one,' Leonie said, 'so I don't know much about my own country. I can hardly speak the language.'

Janie listened as she ate, and registered the fact that Leonie wasn't shy about her nationality, so it was all right to talk about it sometimes.

They were both suddenly excited and eager, wanting to know, wanting to tell, but remembering still to tread warily, and trying to hide it.

The waitress cleared away their plates, and Leonie's manner changed. She seemed almost bored.

'I suppose you know a lot of girls in Manly if you've been there for a few years,' she said, raising her finely arched eyebrows.

What's happened? Janie thought, chilled by the difference. What have I done? She hesitated before answering. It made her miserable. People hate people who haven't got friends, she thought. She won't want to come out with me again.

The return of the waitress with their caramel sundaes gave her time to cover her dismay to some extent. When the waitress had gone Janie said with a laugh, 'Well, no, I don't know many.'

Leonie just said, 'Oh?' on a note that demanded more explanation.

'I was sent to school at Kingslake, you know it, miles out of Manly, and there weren't any other girls from my district there.' Her voice rose unconvincingly, and she laughed again. Afraid of a silence, she went on, 'I just didn't seem to meet any until I went to business college a little while ago.'

Leonie was relentless. 'So you're friendly with the girls from college now?' she said coldly, digging her spoon into her caramel sauce.

Tears pricked Janie's eyes, and she looked angrily at her ice-cream. She couldn't lie; she'd never been able to. Even at a moment like this, the weak, dull, sickly truth had to come.

'Well, I saw some of them on the ferry this morning...' She ate silently until a latent flame of spirit made her ask, 'I suppose you have lots of friends?'

It had been intended to sound careless, indifferent. She would go down fighting, she thought. But her voice was all wrong. She glanced up at Leonie. A calm mask had replaced her bored coldness.

She said in a level tone, 'No, I haven't any friends. I didn't like many of the girls I knew at school, and my best friend went away to Queensland with her family three years ago.'

Wonderful, wonderful Leonie! How can she admit it like that? Because there are two of us? Or because she doesn't care?

Or is it just the way she acts when she does care and doesn't want anyone to know?

Janie allowed herself to relax a little. 'My best friend lives way out in the country, too. I hardly ever see her.'

The waitress brought a tall silver coffee pot to their table, gave them a check and took the dishes.

'Do you like this restaurant, Janie?' Leonie asked as she poured the coffee. Her blue eyes had a new expression, unguarded and vulnerable.

'Oh, yes, I do. We must come here often,' she said, recklessly showing her hand in turn.

For no reason that they could have explained, they both started to laugh, and they looked round at the other diners hoping that they would notice the two attractive girls laughing together, the two friends enjoying each other's confidence, the two lonely Martians meeting unexpectedly on Earth.

The strange silent world of adolescence had exploded, the eggshell walls had collapsed, proclaiming, *You are not alone.* Eyes alight, cheeks flushed, voices bubbling: the questions and answers flew.

'Do you like swimming best?'

'I do!'

'I like nice clothes. I like to read. I like to see plays.'

'The very things that I like.'

'What do you think of grown-ups?'

A sigh, a frown.

'I know. I think so, too!'

No family secrets barred, no holding back from one so close, they thought, and talked and talked, each the best friend of the other.

4
Summertime

It was summertime in Sydney. At about half-past two on a certain Wednesday afternoon Claire Edwards was leaning on the filing cabinet in the office of J. W. Baker's wholesale fashion house. She smiled into the telephone receiver.

'Oh, that's fine. I'll meet you at quarter to six, then, outside the Martinique. Try not to be late,' she cautioned as she had done without success many times before. Her smile deepened to one of indulgent disbelief at Annette's vehement promises of punctuality. 'I believe you. Bye-bye.'

Miss Frazer had come through the door leading from the factory a few seconds before Claire replaced the receiver, and she stood watching the girl, her clear grey eyes noting every fleeting change of expression.

'Annette?' she asked, glancing at the phone. 'What kind of job has she found this time?'

'She's in a fur shop—a furrier's in Double Bay,' Claire answered. 'I'm meeting her after work to hear how she gets on today. I hope she likes it.'

Miss Frazer looked at her watch and sat down at one of the three empty desks in the small office. Paddy, the accountant, was at the bank; Mr Baker was out for the afternoon, she knew. She felt like having a talk and a cigarette.

Claire recognised the signs with feelings of interest and impatience: interest, because in some of her mind she enjoyed these lengthy, emotional chats with Miss Frazer; impatience, because in her fanatical zeal for her job she resented any hindrance to her plans for the afternoon.

'Would you just have a look to make sure the girls are working and bring my bag back when you come, please, dear?' Miss Frazer smiled.

Claire's impatience melted and her heart warmed as it always did under the older woman's direct influence. No one had ever made her feel so appreciated, so efficient, so necessary. 'Of course.' She smiled back, and went through the stockroom to the factory with a swift, haughty, high-heeled walk.

Forty girls were bending over their machines more or less industriously; a few stood at the ironing boards ostensibly waiting their turn to press some small piece of material. Several canvas stands clad in half-finished dresses blocked the narrow passageways between the machines, cutting tables and delivery racks. At the far end of the factory the designers were discussing a difficult new pattern.

Claire's eyes swept over the room, her face stern and, she hoped, reproving. She found Miss Frazer's bag under a pile of soft pink organza and started back for the office. The noise of the machines and the blaring wireless was muffled as the door closed behind her.

'All right?' Miss Frazer raised her thin eyebrows.

'Working away,' Claire said, ignoring the idlers by the ironing boards.

Miss Frazer, who was really Mrs Douglas Preston, lit a cigarette and leaned back in her chair. Apart from her fine skin and large, clear grey eyes she had nothing much, as far as appearance went, on the credit side, except that she dressed well. That magnetism, that charm couldn't come under the heading of appearance, and yet they were so real as to be almost visible.

Everyone knew that hers was an ideal marriage; it had lasted for fourteen years, so far, in a state of extreme harmony. Miss Frazer was naturally reluctant to discuss so intimate a subject as her own married life with many people, but she did mention it to those who were unhappy and came to her with troubles.

It's the least I can do, she thought, to give the poor things a little glimpse of what life can mean when you are loving and beloved.

And so, while she didn't talk about her happiness to many people, most knew about it. It was the kind of news that seemed to circulate. In any case it somehow shone from her.

'Annette's a funny girl,' she began now, her eyes fixed on Claire's. 'What is she again? Hungarian or Polish?'

One must start a conversation in some way and, although Miss Frazer's interest lay more in the rich deep seams of pain, problem, and frustration than in the thin surface soil of mere chatter, she understood the art of mining for such drifts. She'd had practice, of course.

Claire, aware of herself, aware of Miss Frazer and half suspicious of her motives, always responded to her cue and squashed her doubts. It was a stylised game, stimulating and satisfactory, like chess.

'No, she's Estonian,' she said. 'Her mother and father came out here when she was a baby. She doesn't even know the language.'

'They're beautiful stockings you have on today, Claire,' Miss Frazer said as she blew a cloud of smoke into the air. 'Really lovely.'

Claire glowed with pleasure as she glanced down at her long legs.

'Is she a naturalised Australian?' Miss Frazer asked, frowning for a moment at the chipped polish on her thumbnail.

'No, I don't think she's ever bothered about it,' said Claire. 'It costs five pounds or something like that, and you know Annette—she never has any money.'

'If she would stick to one job for a while, she might have,' Miss Frazer said rather tartly.

Annette was a pretty blonde girl whose mother had led her to believe that her looks alone would provide all the necessities and luxuries of life. And, although this belief in the magical properties of a good figure had not so far been justified, Annette's indolent and optimistic disposition made her content to wait for the inevitable. Miss Frazer knew her only through Claire, but she felt slighted by the girl's self-sufficiency.

'How does she get enough money to go out with you?' she asked, feeling that, since it was rather a boring afternoon on the whole, she might as well get to the bottom of Annette.

'Her brother runs a taxi. It was left to him and Annette and her mother when her father died. She gets a share of the takings now and then, and I think they own the house they live in.'

This fact-finding mood of Miss Frazer's always seemed the least attractive side of her to Claire. She wants to know everything about everyone I know, and everything I think, she thought. Claire refused to acknowledge that censorship of principles, opinions, and friends was the price she had to pay for the sympathy and understanding that had become necessary to her.

Miss Frazer ground the butt of her cigarette into the

ashtray and stood up. She smoothed the skirt of her well-cut coffee-coloured dress and picked up her bag.

'Well, she's a silly little girl, Claire. She has some mistaken ideas about life, I think. Although she's been here all her life, it's not the same as having British blood.' Miss Frazer gazed into Claire's eyes. 'I only hope she doesn't pass any of them on to you, dear.'

It was impossible not to feel flattered that Miss Frazer cared about the ideas one had. Claire smiled a reassuring Anglo-Saxon smile.

Rubbing her hands together rather impatiently Miss Frazer said, 'Now I must make a few calls before Paddy comes back from the bank.'

Claire returned to the factory at once, revived and relieved by the noise, warmed by Miss Frazer's goodwill, eager to dispatch her work with even greater efficiency and speed than usual.

A Bing Crosby record was playing. The machinists joined in, concentrating more on the reproduction of Crosby-like voices than on their sewing, Claire thought. But it was a hot afternoon. No one could really blame them. The factory needed air-conditioning to make production rise.

As she bent over the thick invoice book she heard the jukebox in the café downstairs begin to play. The competition spurred the girls to greater efforts and their voices rang out above the whirr of the machines.

Claire worked steadily for the rest of the afternoon, invoicing, answering the phone, interviewing travellers, delighting in the knowledge that she had become a vital part of the firm. I hope Annette has something she likes as well as this, she thought as she ran downstairs just before five-thirty, clinking the keys of the business possessively.

Annette arrived at the Martinique promptly at a quarter to six. 'Hello, honey.' She smiled widely at her friend, and groaned as they went into the bare but atmospheric coffee lounge. 'Wait till I tell you.'

By mutual consent they saved the news for some minutes. Removing their short white gloves with casual deliberation, they studied the menu with the air of detachment they had practised since they were sixteen.

Their order given, they gazed at the other coffee drinkers with bored, haughty faces. Their own reflections were scrutinised even more carefully in a full-length mirror conveniently close to their table.

It gave back Annette's yellow hair, smooth, tanned skin, and wide mouth: a very attractive face. And Claire saw with satisfaction her own beautifully simple black-and-white sleeveless dress, crisp and elegant over a taffeta petticoat. They smiled at one another affectionately.

'Now tell me!' Claire cried, impatient to know Annette's decision. She had always felt that Annette needed guidance and, being blessed herself with sense and intelligence, it was her duty to help Annette choose the right path in life. Theirs had been an ideal friendship for this reason. Claire organised everything, including Annette, and this suited them both.

Annette said, 'It's no good, honey. I just sat out in the shop all day and I was bored stiff. I didn't like the other girl, and the boss expects you to look busy even when there's nothing to do.'

'Oh, Annette, you're always getting bored stiff,' Claire wailed. 'You might like it better tomorrow.'

Annette looked stubborn. 'Well,' she said, choosing her words carefully, 'I might not go tomorrow.'

They were both silent when the waitress brought their order, then Annette went on rather defiantly, 'Otto and some of the boys rang me this afternoon. They're up on leave from the Snowy River and they want me to go round with them while they're here in Sydney for a few days.'

'Who's Otto?'

'He's a Lithuanian. He works in a migrant camp. Remember he came to a party at our place last time he was on leave?'

'No, I don't remember.'

She had never seen Annette's mother or her home or been to one of the many parties that enlivened Annette's existence. They seemed to be very gay affairs, starting round eleven and going on until breakfast time, when the family and the guests would usually go to bed for the day.

Annette had always told Claire that she didn't think

Claire and her mother would like one another, and for that reason she kept them apart. Claire didn't mind about not seeing Annette's mother, but she was sorry that the ban placed parties out of bounds, too.

After one of these sprees Annette would say, 'You wouldn't like it, though. All foreigners.' Her eyes would shine with remembered fun, and Claire would feel, but not say, that there was nothing that she would like better than a party, 'all foreigners'.

Annette's eyes were shining now, and she smiled, showing her beautifully even white teeth. 'I was sure I'd told you about Otto. He was the funny little one who kept saying he loved me.'

Remembering that she was in disgrace for threatening to leave her job, and had no right to be smiling, Annette's high spirits subsided and she concentrated on her meal.

Claire's irritation collapsed in laughter. 'This is good! Cheer up, honey, and enjoy your dinner,' she said. 'You win! But you are a problem. What are you going to do when Otto and his friends go back to work?'

Annette raised her eyebrows and looked indifferent. 'Don't know. I might get another job, or I might just go swimming instead of sitting inside a dreary old fur shop.'

'How much money have you?' Claire demanded.

'About ten shillings.'

'And how much were you to get at this place in Double Bay?'

'About twelve pounds a week.'

Claire asked the waitress for the check. She and Annette wiped their buttery fingers, inspected and repaired their lipstick, and put on their white gloves.

'Where to now?' each asked as they stepped out into the dark warm night.

'Like to go to a show?' Claire said, waving vaguely at the neon signs which flashed restlessly down the length of the street.

Annette's face was rueful. 'Too broke, honey. How about catching a ferry across to Manly and back? You can give me a good lecture and tell me what dear Miss Frazer has been doing today.'

The little thrust at 'dear Miss Frazer' aroused mixed feelings of envy, pity, and annoyance in Claire. Annette laughed at the expression on her face, so that several people passing by looked at them. Claire laughed too, catching Annette's arm and saying, 'Come on, we can just catch this tram down to the Quay.'

'Are my seams straight?' Annette cried anxiously.

Claire dropped a step or two behind her. 'Fine! Now run for the stop.'

They parted at the station later that night on a wave of affection. All was harmony; all was agreed. Annette was going to give work another trial, and report to Claire the following night before going home to see Otto and the boys.

Claire, for her part, saw that Miss Frazer was a 'bit of a menace' as Annette put it, and resolved to withstand her powerful charms. Their thoughts, as they were borne home in opposite directions, turned on one another and their respective tasks for the next day. What a blessing we each speak the same language, they thought. How lucky to get good advice from the right person at the right time.

Mr Baker didn't leave the office all morning, but kept Miss Frazer engaged discussing the new styles for the winter season. He was a fussy little man, by no means unaware of the incandescent sympathy and affection in Mrs Douglas Preston's eyes. He needed his share of the world's understanding as much as anyone, and counted himself lucky in having one of its natural sources in his employ.

After lunch, having unburdened his soul for several hours regarding the business, his family, and his feelings about them, Mr Baker was able to go out into the city, appreciated, vigorous, and refreshed.

Miss Frazer came into the factory when he left and sat down beside Claire, who looked up from the invoice book. The noise of the machines and the wireless made conversation as private as in a confessional chamber.

'Hello, dear,' Miss Frazer sighed. 'What a morning I've had. I thought he'd never go out.'

Claire cleared her throat sympathetically and returned to her book.

'What's the matter, Claire? You don't seem like yourself.' Her voice had a slight edge.

This was an old scene, too, and had its own rigid pattern. Claire determined to break it for once and, she thought, for the last time.

'I'm perfectly all right, Miss Frazer, thanks,' she said, flipping through the prices book.

There was no reply and Claire was mildly horrified by her own presumption in failing to respond to the proffered invitation. As she worked through her list of jobs her heart thumped apprehensively. What would happen next?

After ten minutes of extreme silence, Miss Frazer, not looking at her, said in stifled tones, 'Come through to the office with me please, Claire.'

Picking up her bag she went from the room, her head high, her eyes on the floor.

Claire sighed and put down her pen. She looked around the factory for inspiration to help her through the crisis. One of the machinists, Eloise, caught her eye, her expression inscrutable. Claire looked away and went through to the office. Paddy would be at the bank again, she thought. Oh dear.

Miss Frazer sat facing the door, waiting for her with all the weapons of her powerful personality ready for use. And she was hurt: anyone could see it. Very hurt.

'Now tell me truly, dear. What is the matter with you today?'

Claire's head swam in nightmarish fashion. 'Really, Miss Frazer, nothing's wrong!' she said, trying to sound convincing, for as soon as the words formed, she doubted their fundamental truth. Wasn't life really hollow and pointless? How could life be all right if one was not happy, and who in the world was happy but Miss Frazer and her husband?

'Did Annette upset you last night?' Miss Frazer asked, giving the impression that she would willingly ask every question in the universe if only she might be allowed to solve this problem and remedy its cause.

Claire was momentarily surprised back to reality. 'Annette?' she repeated. 'Oh, no!'

'And yet,' said Miss Frazer, 'your face is strained. There are circles under your eyes, Claire. And you haven't been very nice to me today, you know, though I'm trying to help you, dear.'

How kind she is, thought Claire, wanting to cry. How kind!

'I know that, Miss Frazer,' she said. 'Really, I do. But nothing's the matter.'

Her interlocutor bore the anticlimax gracefully. 'Then if that's true, dear, I'm glad. Just remember that I'm here if you ever need me.' She was silent, watching Claire's averted head, then she smiled gently. 'Look at me, Claire!'

Claire turned reluctantly, and Miss Frazer gazed at her tearful eyes with an involuntary expression of sheer curiosity.

Endeavouring to regain her self-possession, Claire said, 'I'm seeing Annette tonight for a few minutes to hear if she's staying at her job.'

But Miss Frazer's interest had reached its maximum and was declining; her tone was brisk. 'Are you, dear? I don't think that girl has a good effect on you. Now,' she added, 'we'd better do some work before Mr B. comes back.' She turned to the phone and the session was over.

It was hot again, about ninety degrees. Claire felt exhausted. The noise in the factory intensified the heat. She wrote mechanically for the rest of the afternoon, the pen slipping now and then in her hand.

She waited at the Martinique from twenty to six until half-past. Annette was not coming. Claire went home feeling hungry and depressed. Too bad of Annette not to ring to say she couldn't make it, she thought indignantly at intervals until she went to bed.

On Friday, Claire woke with a sore throat and a temperature, and when her mother insisted on phoning the office she didn't feel well enough to protest.

Her room was quiet and she slept for an hour or so, then after having tablets and a hot drink she lay back on the pillows, her head turned to the window. She had a view of tall gum trees on some uncleared land, and down below the slope was the harbour shining in the sun.

The only sounds were the postman's whistle and an occasional car. Inside and outside her room all was quiet, all was warmth and light.

The noise of the telephone in the hall seemed a violation of the morning. Claire pulled a pillow over her exposed ear and continued to study the deep blue sky, but her contemplation was disturbed again.

'It's Annette,' her mother said. 'Will I bring the phone through for you, or will I tell her you'll ring tomorrow?'

'Would you bring it in, please?' Claire asked, shivering a little as she sat up.

'Hello, Annette?'

'It isn't Annette,' the answer came. 'It's her cousin Effie. Annette's here but she doesn't want to speak to you.'

Claire felt a quickening of her senses, a current of alarm. 'Why not? Because of last night?' she asked.

Effie sounded excited. 'Annette was very sorry about letting you down last night and she rang you at work this morning to say so...'

'Well?' Claire's throat was dry.

'Well,' Effie said emphatically, 'she knows now that you've been discussing her with Miss Frazer. You haven't been saying anything good, either, because Miss Frazer gave her a great lecture this morning. Annette's very upset.'

'Oh,' said Claire in an expressionless voice.

'And I told her she shouldn't bother any more with a friend who treats her like that,' Effie said. 'She quite agrees. She doesn't want to meet you ever again.'

'I see,' Claire said flatly.

Effie, prepared for battle, was nonplussed by the enemy's surrender, but after hesitating she shouted, 'Goodbye, then!' and hung up.

Don't think about the future. Don't be lonely or frightened or sorrowful, just yet. Look at the gum trees and the sky. Look at the pattern on the ceiling. Look at the flowers on the dressing table. Don't think about Annette.

The phone rang again.

'Hello?'

'Hello, dear,' Miss Frazer said. 'I've been trying to get you for about ten minutes, but your line's been engaged. How are you feeling now?'

'Not very well.'

'Oh!' There was a pause. 'I won't keep you long. I just wanted you to know that I've had a long talk with Annette. She told me about forgetting to keep her appointment with you last night and I was really annoyed with her. I told her that she didn't deserve a friend like you.' She stopped again. 'Are you there, dear?'

'Yes, Miss Frazer.'

Her voice grew higher and quicker. 'And I took the opportunity of telling her that, since she was lucky enough to be living in this country, the least she could do was to become naturalised and take a job like everyone else. Don't you think I was right, Claire?'

Doubting yourself? Claire wondered. 'I've just had a call from Annette,' she said.

The briefest hesitation. 'Did she apologise to you, Claire?'

'No.'

'I see.' Miss Frazer's voice took on its special note of intimacy. 'She really wasn't good enough for you, dear. I think she has been a bad influence on you.'

'Do you, Miss Frazer?'

'You're not crying, are you, Claire?'

'No, Miss Frazer.' An odd smile tugged at Claire's mouth. 'No, I'm not crying.'

'I'm glad. I won't talk any more now, dear, but we'll have a long chat when you come in to work. I promise you, dear, you're better off without a friend like that.'

'Perhaps you're right.' How easily she said it.

'Then goodbye, darling,' Miss Frazer crooned on her most maternal note.

Claire's eyes were sombre.

'I hope you're a lot better tomorrow.'

'I expect I'll feel fine. Bye.'

Turning to the window Claire saw that the tall, spare gum trees had begun to wave their branches in the warm breeze. The sky was endlessly blue.

A kookaburra's laugh rang out. It lasted for a long time.

It's going to rain, she thought.

5

The North Sea

As soon as my divorce was finalised I went home to Scotland. The weekend after my arrival there, I decided to go away to the east coast for a few days. In a state of over-heightened sensibility, I felt there was something almost incestuous about breathing and eating in the same house as my parents at this particular time. I was embarrassed.

It wasn't that they reproached me. But, as far as I knew, it was the first divorce in our family on either side: a crack had appeared in the solid wall. Of course, I *would* be the one to start the demolition with a hammer and chisel, and a megaphone and my name in the paper.

Looking at my mother and father, I felt guilty. I'd started out so much luckier than either of them, and managed my life so much worse. Dad was a clerk in the civil service and, partly because of the regular transfers all over the British Isles from one small town to another, he and my mother had had a limited and isolated life together.

I was their only child, but it never seemed to me I brought them joy, the way children are supposed to. And, as I grew up, if anyone had asked me what kept them together I'd have said, 'Worries.' They were always in a strange town looking for a house to live in, and it was always winter, so that like the orphans of the storm they had snow falling round their shoulders. When they found a small, usually semi-detached house, it was sometimes empty, sometimes fully furnished, and they either had to store crates of household equipment, or buy the essentials that had been previously provided. All this was perpetually worrying and, of course, the car was fragile when they got it.

Sometimes I was a worry, too, when I was ill, or examinations were due, or scholarships; but then, when the crisis passed, I was laid aside, as it were, with all the receipts for accounts paid.

I remember that several times a week in the summer they'd drive out to the country, which was never far away, and take note of the harvest. As they did this for years, up and down the country, they were in an excellent position to compare districts, yields and methods. If I was home from school I'd sit in the back seat listening: 'John, did you notice that crop of—'

'Yes, he's done well, considering, but do you remember that place in the Borders?' 'You're right, that was better, but then think of the soil!' 'I know, but even so...'

Greek! I'd shrug to myself.

From the stories they told, their meeting and courtship appeared even more than usual to have been a matter of accident. It never occurred to me that they cared much for each other, though I saw they enjoyed these country outings, and they were never bored. And the fact remains, they had been married for forty years, almost to the day, when I first heard someone say, 'She's their divorced daughter from London, Dr Philippa Fraser.'

My father made one comment: 'I don't know what people expect out of life.' This was unanswerable. My mother said, 'Will the publicity hurt you, Pip?'

I pointed out that a divorce could hardly be quieter than ours. There were no blondes, no sensitive dark strangers of either sex, featured in the very unsensational press report. If I'd told them the truth—that the suicide, murder or insanity of one or both of us had been averted by a brief appearance in court—they wouldn't have believed me. ('She always exagger-ates!') No, what they hoped to hear was a conventional expla-nation, involving the customary third party.

After breakfast on Saturday morning, I was drying the dishes when my mother chose to tell me yet again that my father didn't know what people expected out of life. She glanced up in a challenging way, and I was goaded, sickly, into saying, 'Then I'm lucky. When I was ten someone asked me what I wanted to be when I grew up. I said, "Divorced."'

It was then I decided to go away.

My mother's blue eyes stayed on mine, wide open, seeming to understand what I'd meant to do with those words. Her eyes burned away at me, while she breathed through her nose in silence. I was glad to see she'd decided to hate me for the time being. It was an awful thing I'd told her.

'Then I can only say I'm very sorry for Nick, if that's true.'

And I breathed out with relief to see that, after all, she'd turned aside from my blow, leaving all the veils between us intact.

'Sorry. I'm not fit for human company. I'll go over to that place on the east coast for a day or so.'

'I thought you'd just come up *here*,' she said, carefully stacking the plates in the cupboard.

'Sorry.'

The instinct that had carried me from London to this small Scottish village was self-preservation. Never having dealt with this unprecedented situation on my behalf before, instinct seemed to throw up its hands and a hatful of ideas in the hope that I would know best. In coming home, clearly, I hadn't.

It was extraordinarily cold at the station, or perhaps it was just that I'd forgotten Scottish winters in the years down south. Everyone north of the border knows Londoners are soft, effete creatures.

'Don't get out of the car,' I told my parents. 'Hurry home to the fire. It's much too miserable to wait round on platforms.'

They eyed me, disappointed. It was almost a year since I'd last seen them, and here I was rushing off already. 'All right, Pip, we've gone. Take care of yourself, there's a good girl.'

They looked a bit shabby, and really quite old, I was alarmed to see. I clutched the car door wondering what I could do to make it up to them. When we'd left the house I'd given them a cheque—something quite substantial, and anyway they were perfectly all right! So why did I want to cry in front of these familiar strangers who said such irritating things to me, and made me feel I shouldn't know the facts of life at thirty? I was maudlin. It was ridiculous!

'You're a great one for trains,' my mother said. 'Always rushing away to school, or university, or London.'

'Oh, choof off, both of you! When I come back we'll see some shows in Edinburgh, and have dinner at the North British every time, too.'

So they went away laughing in a scandalised fashion at the thought of such extravagance, and the fact that their girl Pip had threatened to provide it, and undoubtedly would.

But then I was in the train and there I was no one's daughter; all I was was someone conscious of error. I'd always been so clever! It was almost comical to think of this very worthy IQ bending its powers to the ancient problem of choosing and being chosen by a mate, and coming up with a mistake like this…

'The North Sea,' I told the taxi driver. My face had frozen on the walk from the train, and it was physically difficult to speak. My chin was paralysed.

'Is it Mr and Mrs Byrne's place you're wanting?' the old man asked, turning around.

'I don't know. The North Sea. It's a private hotel. Someone recommended it a few years ago.'

'Och, aye, it's the Byrnes' place you're wanting. They've been in it now for about two year.' He had a thick Scots accent and bright grey eyes.

'All right, the Byrnes' place. I'd like to arrive in time for dinner.'

'Och, there's no hurry for your dinner, lassie. You've missed that by a half-hour at least. Still, they'll not let you go to your bed without a cup of tea.'

This was all very charming. My capacity for making mistakes was obviously in its early stages. I could see myself headed for a long career in the manufacture of mistakes. *Dame Philippa Fraser* would appear in some future New Year's Honours List, her title bestowed by the sovereign for her unremitting efforts to raise the standard of mistakes throughout the country, single-handed.

'Och, they've let it go down, the old place,' the driver said confidentially. 'Irish, you know.'

'Oh?'

'*She's* Irish!' he assured me, turning right round again and nodding. 'She's a hard worker, too, but him! Never does a hand's turn about the place. The leaves are all over the gardens and up the drive. You wait. I'll have to change gear to get over them all.'

There was a lack of logic somewhere in his tale that worried me, as trivial things now had the power to do. But it stayed in the background with everything else while my attention listened to Nick, Nick, Nick, Nick…Nothing but a name, but it said everything, ticking in my head the way it had for months.

The old man went on, very dry. 'Of course, Mr Byrne's got to entertain the guests.' ('En-tairr-tain,' he said.)

It was too dark to see the square stone house or the dunes of leaves around it when we pulled up.

'Come along in,' said Mrs Byrne as the taxi drove off. 'Willie's an old chatterbox. This is your room, Miss Fraser. There'll be supper in the sitting room at nine, and there's a fire in there, so when you've unpacked you might like to come through and meet the other guests. Just Mr and Mrs Alston. He's an artist from London. And the bathroom's just across the hall here. You may find this tap hard to manage, but it isn't really. So now I'll leave you to unpack. Oh yes, a shilling meter for the radiator. You'll need it tonight.'

The Irish Mrs Byrne was small, compact, hard-eyed. She looked not well disposed towards the world or its inhabitants.

I debated going straight to bed, but I'd eaten so little all day that even tea and a biscuit began to seem desirable, and I was leaving my room to face the strangers when I heard someone shout, 'No, I'm sorry! I'm not in the mood to discuss knitting with some maiden lady from the Borders!' And a door opened onto the dark hallway showing a lighted room out of which stumbled a thin, bearded man. He sheered away from me, not looking, and belted downstairs.

A woman with dark hair calmly followed him out. 'Colin…Oh, good evening.' She smiled at me, and waved an arm towards the stairs. 'My husband.'

So these were the Alstons. The artist. The Artiste! I thought unkindly. A sensitive Artiste, too! Above all mankind I disliked my fellow sufferers. What a boring, despicable crew they were the world over, having 'breakdowns', and bravely recovering, or else not…

A brass standard lamp and a coal fire lighted the low-ceilinged room labelled Guests Only. A girl in a green dress stood at a trolley pouring tea.

'Hello. I'm Mrs Byrne's daughter, June. This is my husband, Cliff, and that's the baby. It hasn't got a name yet, though it's being christened tomorrow. And this is Pepper.'

She crouched in front of the brown-and-white terrier at her feet, and fed him a biscuit, bite by bite, then stood up, flipping back her fair hair with her hand. 'How do you like your tea, Miss Fraser?'

Cliff, the young man, held the baby awkwardly, trying to drink his tea; his wife seemed rather pointedly not to notice. He was in his early twenties, white-skinned and sick-looking. Eventually his clumsiness, something, provoked me into taking the baby while he finished his supper. It was a young baby, about six weeks old, a little girl.

June looked on indifferently when Cliff took her back again from me, and said, 'You'd better come to her christening tomorrow, if you can be bothered. Mother said to ask you. They won't light the fire till we all get home from church, so you might as well.'

Who was I to resist such an invitation? 'I'd enjoy that,' I said. 'What are you going to call her?'

'It hasn't got a name,' she said brusquely. 'I told you.'

'I didn't realise…'

'I think we might call her June, after her mother,' the young husband said, but his wife's eyes moved from the baby to the dog in a sort of venomous silence. She said suddenly, 'What's *your* name?'

'Philippa.'

'We'll call it that.'

Cliff looked up, then down, resignedly, at the baby's small

bare feet. They were cold: I'd noticed when I held her. She was far from warmly dressed, and the room was draughty. Outside it was starting to rain. I decided to leave this luckless child and its parents to their own company.

'What will you have for breakfast?' the girl called after me.

'Coffee and rolls. Something like that.'

'Right. I'll tell Mother.' And she looked at me with envy. I was not Cliff's wife. I was not Philippa's mother.

No, indeed! And how enviable I was, lying awake, staring at the wall, hearing that name, my mind disordered by it, wanting nothing, feeling nothing, believing nothing.

In the morning Mrs Byrne lingered over the delivery of the breakfast tray. 'So, the baby's to be called after you! She should never have had it, that's the trouble. She's a clever girl, June. She could have got a grant and gone to university. (That's what *I* should have done, too, years ago!) Her headmistress wanted it, and her father and I did. But she met Cliff at a youth hostel in the Highlands one weekend and within four months they were married. I should've let her meet more boys. He's been sick the whole time, all in his imagination, I think. He works in the post office in a mining village. They'll go home there after the christening. What sort of life she's let herself in for… Is that enough butter for you? We'll leave for the church at quarter past ten.'

Mr Byrne, a fake-hearty, lantern-jawed Scot, drove us in a

fifth- or sixth-hand Daimler to a small stone church set in one of Scotland's countless grassy hollows. There wasn't a cottage in sight, just a few sheep chewing blandly.

The Alstons, at the last moment, had been asked to act as godparents, and had not refused. But I noticed Colin Alston's expression during the ceremony, and saw that a hand or a foot tapped compulsively under the strain of this ordeal. He seemed very tense, but he and his wife, Marion, were pleasant people, and I guessed they were sorry about the outburst the night before that I had been bound to overhear.

Back at the North Sea the new Philippa was placed on the floor by the fire, and Pepper yelped about the room, jealous of her, sniffing her face, investigating. I wanted to protest, but didn't. The baby cried. Pepper dozed by the fire, winking at it, half-awake.

When June noticed this, she flew to him and picked him up. 'You mustn't look at the fire, sweet, and make your eyes hot. It's bad for them.' She kissed his nose, then went away to collect her remaining bags and baskets while her father revved up the engine to drive them to the station. I stood at the front door with the Alstons to see them go off. Mr and Mrs Byrne were waiting in the front seat while Cliff and June tossed rugs and overnight bags into the back.

'Cliff, here's a rattle for the baby. There wasn't much choice in the shop.' Marion went over to the window of the car with a pink plastic rattle. 'I'm afraid it isn't very nice.'

'Look, June! Little Pip's first present,' he cried, smiling.

'Oh yes,' she said, and rattled the thing before the baby's face as they drove off through the leaves, past the crumbling stone pillars at the gateway.

In the afternoon Mrs Byrne rested while her husband and Colin Alston went walking by the sea. I stayed beside the fire, and so did Marion Alston, with a book and a cigarette. We talked a bit instead of reading. By half-past two, without a light, it was too dark to see the printed page. By half-past three, the misty, dank and penetrating winter night had settled in. We had been silent for a minute or so, sunk in the profound silence of the house, when Marion said, as if she'd taken a decision, 'Colin enjoyed talking to you at lunchtime. He very seldom discusses painting now, so it excited him. That's why he went out with Mr Byrne.'

'I see.' I *had* wondered.

Marion said, 'He was married once before, you know, almost twenty years ago. The girl died soon afterwards. Colin knew her for six months. He's never quite recovered.'

'Have you been married long?'

'No, quite a short time.'

'It might make a difference to him.'

'It might. It might be too late. He's forty-five. He used to be a promising young painter. I read about him in London and saw his work long before I met him. Now he calls himself a competent hack. He does work he despises.' She shrugged.

'There's nothing wrong with competence, and we eat well. The only sad thing is—he was capable of more, and lucky, recognised, encouraged…But he just—gave up the ghost. Or rather—didn't.'

While she looked at the flames of the fire I looked at her hair, and the streaks of grey in it, and I opened my mouth, and closed it. I should say something. But what? I could think of nothing at all. I leaned back in my chair as empty of words, of sympathy, as physically feeble and helpless, as that young baby setting out in life so heavily handicapped.

And it occurred to me as I sat, tired with the effort of drawing one shallow breath after another, that this feeling of bloodlessness, toothlessness, of having had so many qualities drawn off that I was strange to myself, was becoming more and more familiar. And in a way I loved being this weak, indifferent woman.

But why was I being subjected to these sights and stories? Hadn't I taken three months' leave of absence from my practice in London to escape them? Down there, if all those patients had been content with a little less—as much as they paid for and were entitled to!—I'd have stayed on. I was not eager to pass twelve weeks, eighty-four days and nights, without the distraction of work. But at least half of them came to say, in effect, 'Doctor, I'm unhappy. Help me. What do I do now?'

It's all there in any government handbook describing the medical services—the number of patients seeking treatment for symptoms of psychosomatic origin. I used to be interested in these people—I can't think why. A year ago, of course, I was that much younger, that much more credulous and ignorant...

All at once I felt oppressed and angry. People telling you sad stories! But then Marion Alston looked over at me, and somehow I was confused. Perhaps it was the effect of the firelight, or the darkness, or the silence, but I seemed to catch sight of a surprising strength of spirit in her. I wondered if, minutes before, when I was so resentful, she hadn't been offering, rather than asking for, help.

'My husband and I were divorced recently, and I don't seem to be very well.'

This statement was roughly the length of Pericles' funeral oration when compared with my total silence on the subject with my closest friends and relations.

Marion said nothing. I began to feel humiliated. Had I been mistaken in my intuition of her strength? Was she as speechless as I had been? She was older than me, about fifteen years older. (How dreadful! She had actually had to survive fifteen years longer than...)

'I don't seem to know what to do next,' I said.

'No. But at least you will have a better idea of what not to do.'

'You mean—poor Cliff and June?'

'And the Byrnes, and Colin and me.'

'You've come through,' I said. 'Anyone can see. But the others…The circumstances are so different, I don't…'

'Nevertheless,' Marion said, 'there aren't unlimited roads out of these situations.'

What did she mean? I said, 'You came through.'

She picked up a burning cinder with the tongs and threw it back on the fire. 'Yes. But a few years ago I'd have served as a warning to anyone. Though it mightn't have been all that obvious at first sight.'

'How?' I insisted. I felt shameless, but I had to know what she knew.

'I was very gay, but there just wasn't much of a person to be any more. Nothing mattered, though, so that didn't matter either. I had no reason not to be bright. I went to too many parties, and sometimes drank too much. I carefully had no time to think or read. Some of the music and pictures and plays and books I'd admired for years turned morbid and dull, but it didn't matter.'

'What were you doing?'

'Congratulating myself on my survival, I suppose. At the time I didn't see how little it amounted to.'

'And did you meet Colin then?' I thought, There's always a stock solution to other people's problems—in this case, another man.

She shook her head. 'This was years before I knew him.'

Outside on the landing there were voices, and the chinking

of teacups. Mrs Byrne came in trundling the trolley, and her husband and Colin Alston followed.

'What timing!' they said. 'Teatime! We knew when to get back.'

'How's that fire? Oh, George, I thought you'd look after it while I was resting this afternoon.'

'Aye, well...I'd better get on with the leaves after tea,' said George Byrne, lowering himself into his large easy chair for the remainder of the day.

'We know all about that,' said his wife, handing round cups and plates.

'You were both extremely wise to stay in all afternoon,' Colin told Marion and me, standing over us. 'I have never seen a more cheerless sight than that stretch of water out there.' He tugged at his beard, smiled down nervously, then sat beside us to talk about painting, his foot tapping relentlessly all the while.

We all parted friends. It was left that I should get in touch with the Alstons when I returned to London. While Colin paid their account next morning, I stood with Marion watching for the taxi. She buttoned her coat up.

I tried to make a joke of it by laughing a bit, but I had to say, in a low voice, 'For heaven's sake, Marion, don't go without telling me the end of your story. Yesterday you had to stop halfway. I still don't know what to do.' I despised myself as I would have despised one of my patients, now that I was this new person. My tact, my finesse, my hobnailed boots, astonished me, but speak I would and did.

Marion looked through the door and away from the house. She seemed grave. 'If it was anything simple, Philippa, would Colin be like this? I don't know what happened. I changed. I could never remember how.'

I watched her.

She said, 'In any case, if I could tell you, if it could be contained in a sentence, it would no longer be true. It would alter. Neither of us would understand. There are some—apprehensions—that are loaned out occasionally and withdrawn as soon as used. Do you...?'

I waited.

She said, 'People do come through. It helps to want to.'

I was not pleased.

They drove away by taxi to the station, and I stood with the Byrnes on the step and waved. After that I went straight out and bought a soft lemon-coloured lamb for the baby, and some postcards. Mrs Byrne gave me June's address and I wrapped up the parcel, and wrote the cards to my mother and father, though I would probably reach home before they arrived. I sent cheques to Edinburgh for theatre tickets for the following week. And, lastly, I wrote a letter to Nick to say goodbye and wish him well.

When I had posted all this, I walked back from town to

the North Sea. Coming up the drive empty-handed, I saw Mr Byrne in the doorway looking out at the leaves. I called to him, 'What about a joint attack? There are two rakes here. If you start over that side, and I start here, we could make a great clearance by teatime. And it's dry, and there's hardly any wind.'

'You're right!' he exclaimed. 'It's the day I've been waiting for!' And he dashed for the rakes and brought mine across, loping over the drifts. 'These leaves are a sore point with Mrs Byrne, you know. This'll surprise her. Och, anyway, there's nothing like a bit of exercise if there's a body to keep you company.'

This is childish, I thought angrily. This is stupid. And I didn't want to do it, any more than I'd wanted to move all morning, or write that letter, or buy that lamb, or sign my name. What a way to try to make life bearable! Who *had* that woman thought she was—the priestess of Apollo delivering oracles?

Still, we kept on, and we swept up the leaves.

6

The Cornucopia

Julia Holt was never impressed. Not being impressed, indeed, was one of the chief things about her. Any new friend who ran to her with news, like a pup prancing up with a mouldy bone between its teeth, learned this. The new friend, as it were, fell back a step or two in an effort to bring the whole of Julia into focus again, while Julia looked knowing and laughed, almost accusing her of lying.

Protestations—'But, Julia, I *am* flying round the world with Toby'—were beside the point. Julia hadn't doubted it for an instant. She doubted *nothing*. *Yes*, Harry had been elected captain of his school. *Yes*, Grace had won first prize in the lottery. *All right*, the stars of the Old Vic touring company had accepted invitations to Edna's party, and *yes*, Nancy and

Stewart were dining with the governor-general. *Okay. All right. Very well.*

'You knew already, Julia! Someone told you!'

But no one had. And yet there was no mistaking Julia's extreme lack of interest in world tours and vice-regal dinners. Her lovely eyes roamed the most distant prospect available to them, moved, dully persecuted, across the skyline from east to west. No concert pianist obliged to support herself by rearing chickens, rounding them up for the night, could have seemed more disengaged than she. It was dispiriting to Julia's new friend. Caught up by the thrilling news just delivered—to Julia *first*, before everyone—she was not sufficiently detached to find comfort in the thought that this tone of voice brought out the buried Australian in Julia.

Up at the end of every remark her voice went, in that unconsciously tentative way that makes the most affirmative statement sound like a question. It is irritating when people seem not absolutely certain even of their own names.

No, but *if* Julia *did* believe and still looked so amused and pitying, it could only mean that she had secrets beside which her new friend's offerings were paltry indeed. Her friend felt discontented, dashed. What was the use? What was life all about, anyway?

Then, just at this awful moment, wonderfully, Julia noticed and declared the most spontaneous and tremendous admiration for, say, her new friend's nylon stockings, her hand-stitched gloves, her gold earrings or the colour of her hair.

This free gift of herself was so unexpected that it threw Julia's friend off balance. With a shrill little laugh she protested and wriggled and twisted her admired hands and legs, like a tiny pampered lapdog yapping fiendishly and chasing her own tail.

This sort of incident, which occurred over and over in Julia's life, always featured one of her Grade II friends. Her *equal*, Grade I friends were, without exception, notable people who had hung in society's sky long before Julia herself was hailed by astronomers. These Grade II girls were, strictly speaking, protégées, the hoity-toity daughters of earthy butchers, or pretty secretaries living in two-bedroomed bungalows, learning about etiquette and hygiene and make-up from teenagers' weeklies. They married young men who'd left school at fifteen and entered insurance offices and finance companies, studying their product—money—from the ground up. Now, to the astonishment of relations and old neighbours, these youthful couples were rich.

Julia Holt had belonged to this caste once herself, but uncanny natural qualities, ten years' advantage in age, and Ralph's exceptional flair for finance had put her in a category of her own. She was an example to them all.

What inspired the Grade II protégées was the impossibility of impressing Julia. Her sophistication was immense. The odd smart aleck would sometimes throw names and words at her in an exasperated attempt to wrench a reaction: Tolstoy, Chartres, Frank Lloyd Wright, mother, Casals, concentration camps, the Parthenon, love, Gandhi, bomb, the Marx Brothers…

One of Julia's eyebrows disposed of them all. She was like a bronze idol, impervious to life's trials. The possibility that her imperviousness might extend into the territory of life's joys occurred to no one. For the second most striking thing about Julia was the amount of happiness she possessed. (It was usual to think of Julia's happiness as something owned, rather than experienced.) She wore it like an aphrodisiac.

Julia and Ralph Holt…Regarding their wealth, they would only say in a modest fashion, 'Well, we'll always have three meals a day.' Modesty in regard to their marriage, however, which was a legend in Sydney society, would have seemed hypocritical. The Holts were generous with their private life, displaying, discussing, analysing it with humanity and wit. Even Ralph, a man with many large transactions on his mind and not a conversationalist at all, took time off to contribute a description. Together he and Julia sang a kind of hymn to their happiness.

Ralph Holt was remarkable as any man must be to leave school at fifteen and turn from farm boy to delivery boy to office boy to millionaire at the age of forty. Now money, Julia, and their two sons were his entire life. While his family naturally came first, he did *feel* for money: it was his Rosetta Stone.

(The boys, Peter and Paul, were twins, aged nine. Ralph doted on them. Julia doted, too, she *worshipped* them: it was just that she saw their defects rather clearly. Julia had never *wanted* children. Her life had been perfect. Who but a fool would have tried to improve on it? But there was some mischance. She was pregnant and Ralph wanted a son. To call that period of her existence nightmarish, ghastly beyond belief, would be a ludicrous understatement. Only Ralph and her doctor had the least inkling of what her feelings were then, and they had sworn to forget the episode forever.)

Ralph's great appeal for his fellow man was that, though he was rich, he treated everyone the same. He wasn't a bit arrogant. He never bullied. Away from head office he was good-natured, easily led, easily diverted, even soft. He evinced the universal balloon-like simplicity that humans display when temporarily bereft of their vocations. Unplugged from his niche in the gymnasium of circumstance, he was like a horse in an aeroplane.

It was Ralph's boast that good luck hadn't altered him, but in connection with money one gradual change *had* overtaken him. Whereas in his youth he had spent carelessly, he was now inclined to go through the house at night switching off lights. He'd been known to walk in the rain rather than hail a taxi, and there was the story Julia told against him about a box of cakes.

Valerie Turner, a Grade III girlfriend of Julia's, one of the disciples, had been deputed to buy and deliver some cake from the patisserie. Before she reached the shop she was knocked down by a car on a pedestrian crossing, and she had to send Julia an apology from hospital. She felt awful about inconveniencing Julia, but her leg had been hurt and the doctor insisted she stay in bed. So what could she do?

'Don't worry! I'll call Ralph,' Julia said. 'He can get one of the juniors to collect them and then bring them home himself this evening.'

When Ralph walked in the door with the cake box, his eyebrows were up among his hair, and his mouth was wide open with the pressure of throttled speech just waiting for Julia's presence for release.

'What do you think these things cost? I used to *like* them. What do they think they're made of? What do they think *we're* made of? It's just eating money!'

Ralph had no time for games or hobbies. He read the financial papers. He understood world affairs insofar as they affected the stock markets, and prayed for governments to rise and fall to the advantage of his company's holdings. He was mildly indifferent to his personal appearance, feeling no pressure to spend inordinately on clothes. The arts embarrassed him the way churches did. Julia could take an interest in both as long as *he* was not invited to watch male ballet dancers cavorting like a lot of ——, or to be earbashed by some lecherous old ——. (Ralph rarely used unpleasant language.)

He belonged to the best clubs. He and Julia attended all

the state dinners, balls and receptions in honour of visiting royalty, and while Ralph cursed these social duties he had to admit that it was only fitting that the people who amounted to something should congregate to pay and receive a quota of homage.

Really, he enjoyed high life. He enjoyed dancing with Julia and her girlfriends (Ralph was apt to identify other women as Julia's girlfriends, rather than as the wives of their husbands), and talking over dinner to politicians and knights, some of whom, these days, were inclined to defer to him.

It wasn't that Ralph felt unkindly towards the men he had met on his climb to the top. He could recall one or two fishing mates who were more *congenial* than some of his daily associates. But he was wise enough to know how impossible friendship with them was. Small men always hoped for some advantage. They would want to pick his brains, ask advice, expect him to use his influence and find jobs for relations. Without thinking twice, Ralph directed his favours to men of his own stature.

There was a party one night at his and Julia's place, and Zelda Burton, the wife of a bright youngster in the company, crashed the men's end of the room to harangue them about some tragic event in the life of her housekeeper, Molly. From *their* end of the room, the other wives watched coldly. 'Zelda *must* be with the men, have you noticed? *Our* company doesn't mean a thing to Zelda.'

'I'll go to the rescue, if you're worried.' Julia laughed, her voice tender and teasing. 'Wait a sec! Fear not!' Off she went...

'And poor Molly's been starving herself to pay off her sewing machine,' Zelda was saying. 'She makes overalls at night for some clothing factory. She's got too many kids and her husband's a no-hoper, and she's had to pay *twice* the regular price for her machine because of the interest to our company.'

All the men grinned sheepishly except Zelda's husband and Ralph.

Julia said drily, '*I* think your Molly should have her head examined.'

Everyone laughed, but Zelda insisted: 'Some people have rotten luck, though, Julia. She was sick for years after the Depression from malnutrition, and *now*—' Zelda was impassioned, her dark eyes big.

Julia smiled. Her eyelids drooped. 'Really? *Malnutrition?*'

The listeners gaped, then gasped and gave a shout of laughter as her innuendo struck them like some gorgeous, shocking snowball.

A mistress of Zen, Julia! Illumination! Obviously, Molly was a fraud. Obviously, old Zelda had been knocking back more Scotch than was good for her.

'Now, look, my sweet,' Julia was saying. 'Who *makes* your Molly woman pay the price of two machines for one? Who twists her arm? I'm not saying she's not a fine character! But she just hasn't got the nous to think it out, and save up, and buy the damn thing outright. Now, isn't that true? And isn't she also starving herself to pay for clothes for these kids of hers?'

Undermined, but still frowning at the mild-faced, milky men, Zelda said, 'But the point is...When *my* kids wanted a machine to play at making dresses in the school holidays, we got one through the company *half*-price.'

Holding glasses, standing in strategic formation, the men were fascinated. Though the sum of money involved was too trivial, it was, nevertheless, *money*, and the whole story began to symbolise some problem, to involve principles...By the instant, they grew harder.

'Just keep her out of the files,' Ralph joked. 'That's all I ask.'

With her usual aplomb, Julia was leading Zelda to her proper place among the ladies. Back they went together across the parquet floor, past the new portrait of Julia, the windows, and the roses, into female territory.

'But, Julia, it's *hell* finding someone to replace a worker like Molly. She used to *slave* for me. I'm just so miserable—'

With her eyes fixed on the women they approached, Julia was saying, 'Yes, yes, but if you're worried about her dying of hunger, get on the phone and order a hamper to go to her house. That's what I did when Mrs Whatnot went to hospital, and she adored it. It made a great impression in the ward.'

The other wives remembered how generous Julia had been to Mrs Whatnot, who had rather ungraciously died just the same.

'You sent blankets, too, before they took her away,' Rose Lewis reminded her.

'Oh, God, yes! Ralph thought I was mad. He kept asking me for a handout. He kept saying, "Got any spare tenners today, lady?"'

Poor Ralph! The cleverest thing he ever did was marry Julia. He confessed that she knew as much about the workings of the company as he did himself. He discussed everything with her. God alone knew what he would have made of himself without her!

Julia was realistic about these things: she was superior to Ralph. He knew it. She knew it. How could she act the little woman? If she had been a *man*, if she had even been a *woman* (of course she *was*), she would have run rings round Ralph, *and* every other…Ah, well!

There were ways in which Ralph and Julia had grown alike. For instance, money was nearly the most alluring topic of conversation in the world, especially for Julia when her Grade III girlfriends, the disciples, were about. With a rakish grin and an expression of mock terror, she'd cry, 'I've just spent three hundred guineas on three dresses. Ralph'll murder me!'

The girls always exclaimed, and looked envious and horrified and proud of her. If they ever reflected that three hundred guineas were to Ralph what three pennies were to them, they never said so.

The first two questions Julia asked potential disciple material were, 'How much do you make?' and 'How much have you got in the bank?' She knew how poverty-stricken the members of her Grade III contingent were. Alice Wright was a typical example: fortyish, faded, and single. She lived alone in one room, and had no family. Out of her salary she saved four pounds a week, which wasn't easy, and therefore had two hundred and eight pounds a year to represent security, to spend on clothes, cosmetics, holidays, insurance, Christmas presents, doctors, dentists, eiderdowns, coffee percolators, entertainment, chocolate bars and headache tablets. Moreover, she wanted very much to visit Europe one day, so her savings stood for hope, as well. When she confided this dream to Julia one night, mistiming it, Julia said a little cruelly, 'What are you going to use for money?'

It was a tiny flaw in Julia that she resented, seemed—impossibly!—almost jealous of, any sign of initiative or individual desire on the part of her girlfriends. But it was only that she didn't want to lose them. After all, she had acquired these companions, one by one, over the years, by a process of most intense and flattering cultivation. They'd found themselves unutterably charmed that Julia Holt was moved by the secrets of their small lives. And now they were lucky to live vicariously through her. Only Julia had need of them, Julia, whose life was so rich in events that she needed all their help to cope with it.

'Sweetie, *would* you slip out of the office at lunchtime and get those satin shoes from that French dyeing place?'

'*Can* you get my pearls out to me before a quarter-past six, lamb? They're fixing the clasp at Huntley's. I must have them tonight.'

'Darling, *would* you go and look after old Auntie Win for me this weekend? You can go straight from work on Friday. *I* can't very well leave Ralph and the boys, and she'd hate a nurse, and she's pretty sick—or she thinks she is! Someone has to be there. You haven't got anything else fixed, have you? Because if you have, I can easily get Kate, or Brenda, or Valerie, to go along for me.'

When Ralph had to travel interstate and Julia curtailed her social life, the faithful disciples came into their own. Out to the North Shore they went as soon as summoned, and along the dark avenue to the beautiful house. Like equals, they relaxed with Julia in front of the television screen and, under disen-chanted expressions, half-swooned with the relief of being safe and warm within solid walls, in a lamp-lit room where every artefact was what it seemed to be. The wood was flawless and polished by hand; the roses were home-grown and hanging, heavy, from silver bowls.

While they watched the screen and smoked, and drank their whisky, Julia chatted about local scandals, her small staff and the price of grapes. If it happened that she was con-strained, en route to some homely subject, to refer to her new sables, or the two new paintings chosen by that eminent art-critic man whom, unfortunately, there was less time now to see, or to some titled personages who were Grade I bosom friends, it was not that Julia had any desire to stir up envy. On the contrary, it distressed her that Kate (or Alice, or Brenda, or Valerie) should make a fuss.

'What's *who* like?' she would repeat after them with a repressive frown and a small pained movement of her hand. 'Oh, *him*…Oh, all right.'

Naturally, the girls had no news of any consequence. But if Kate, for instance, being present, could shed light on some suspected weakness in Brenda, being absent, Julia was warmly responsive. She adored human nature. She saw through people so easily, she should have been a psychologist.

When the pre-dinner drink or two were disposed of, Julia and her companion strolled through to the kitchen to see what Elsie, the cook, had concocted for them. In front of the screen again, with the coffee table holding the huge tray ('Let's rough it tonight!'), they ate and drank and lounged against cushions.

'More? Oh, go on! You know you'd like to.' Smiling and frowning at her in an odd, critical way, Julia heaped another spoonful of curry onto her friend's plate. For no reason, Julia gave a short frustrated laugh. But second helpings are often a disappointment. Julia was conscious that this same Kate (or Alice, or Brenda, or Valerie) would have been dining at home tonight on boiled eggs, or frozen fish fingers, or a single lamb chop with a tomato, and finishing with Nescafé and a sweet biscuit.

The knowledge caused Julia a confused sort of suffering. She didn't *mind* Kate eating her dinner...It was only that she was afraid that she was sinning against her own kind, that she was harbouring anarchists and revolutionaries.

But, in justice, as she quickly reminded herself, the girls never tried to take advantage of her position. It was one of the really lovely things about them that they never expected help from her though they did long to entertain her in return, in their bedsitting rooms, buying in her special brand of Scotch and coping with casseroles swimming in cream and herbs as well as their funny little ovens allowed. But Julia was never free. When Ralph was away, it was bliss to snatch a quiet evening at home. 'Yes, I *will* truly come to your place next time, but look, lamb, you're flat out at the office all day. Elsie here can knock us up a bite, and we can put our feet up and watch quizzes on TV like a couple of old maids.'

How could they mind? She was charming. She was their claim to fame, their connection with life. Charm and Julia were synonymous to all who knew her. She admitted herself that, without her charm, she and Ralph would have been merely part of the Grade II crowd. As this was Australia, where millionaires tended to be less exclusive and eccentric than in most other countries, left to himself Ralph would not have known how to be exceptional. Julia just *was*.

*

Every now and then, as a sort of change of diet, Julia would invite some junior university men to an informal dinner. 'You'll just have to take us as you find us!' she'd say, laughing a warning.

Frankness can be enchanting, especially in the rich. It seems so unnatural in them.

'Come and sit next to me, John. Leave those old business-men to bore each other.' With a thoughtful, almost intimate expression she would watch him, her young expert.

Patting his tie and smiling and blinking at Mrs Holt—Julia—who was not bad-looking for her age (about thirty-seven?), John approached.

The way she looked at him, with such extreme unwavering attention, it was obvious that she was interested. Wasn't it? Now that he was beside her on the sofa, blandly staring back—he *was* a good ten years younger than the woman and could afford to be bland, let's face it!—she even put a hand on his, warmly.

No. Instantly, he realised that she'd done it as an older woman innocently would. It was sweet. He had misjudged the situation altogether. She smelled marvellous. Her make-up was very pretty, though she naturally had a few lines on her face.

'Now, what's all this?' she asked with a troubled sincerity like nothing he'd encountered in his life before. 'Just what is all this about India?'

Wonderful woman! Out of the whole room, she had picked the one person who could tell her.

'I can say this much—' John began.

A minute later she interrupted him reproachfully, half-laughing. 'Darling, darling. I'm an intelligent woman, I hope, but make it a little easier for me. I'm not a scholar, you know, and I don't pretend to be.'

Oh! Her eyes looked so deeply into his, and were so blue, and seemed to mean, to suggest...John condensed his encyclopaedic knowledge of the problems of India into three wise sentences. For her part, Julia seemed to learn them word for word; more, seemed to grasp the exciting ramifications, implications, the whole complex of thought that lay behind them. Rarely had his perceptions been so acutely appreciated.

When Harry Grieve was cornered by her lovely boisterous blue gaze he didn't object at all. He looked at her speculatively over his glass, and Julia said, 'What's all this about Greek sculpture? No, seriously, Harry. I want to know. There's a museum at Delphi, they tell me—'

She was right! There was! There is! Harry's expression altered. She smelled marvellous. Her make-up was smooth and pearly, though she bore those visible traces of preservation that were natural and becoming to her age. Her way of searching your eyes was not so much provocative as—well, yes, it *was* provocative.

Julia listened to Harry's wise sentences.

The distinguished men she met, about whose interests *Who's Who* was so helpful, were delighted to hear the subjects closest to their hearts—India, Greek sculpture, geology, fishing, the United Nations, cricket—receiving such sensible attention from this good-looking society woman. Now she was appealing to the company for support. What ignoramuses! She was the only one at the table who knew anything about it!

A certain look and two or three smart words she'd learned the week before were enough to convince them all that she knew what they were talking about. And *cared*. These were the world shakers, were they? Internationally known. And she, *she*, little Julia Holt had tricked them.

These formal occasions were all very well, but Julia much preferred an evening at home with a few handpicked visitors from abroad. She loved new people. The Holts diverted them with tales about associates and acquaintances whom the newcomers would soon number in their circle. *Someone* had to give these lambs the lowdown. It was only fair.

'Oh, you can tell a mile off they commit incest,' Ralph would say with his gentle smile. 'Ask Julia. She's got an instinct for these things.'

'Blanche and her son? Listen, sweeties, it's quite common. You know it is.'

Of course they did.

As eyes slid, full of glee, from one face to another, saluting their own kind now that they were *certain*, Ralph would continue with his revelations. He still had the placid country face of a farm boy, which added a peculiar piquancy to the night. 'Of course, James and Martha—we think they're both queer.'

'Well, they *are*. No *think* about it. And then—'

Once Julia started ticking them off on her fingers, there was really no end to the newsworthy misdemeanours their friends were guilty of. Obscenity was everywhere! Like spies they searched it out, exchanging clues, drawing inferences, inventing hilarious episodes for their private amusement. It was all good fun, and livened their small parties wonderfully.

If human beings were automatically rendered ideal, creatures of the highest order, as a result of successful sexual relations, the Holts should have been enshrined in a mountain grotto somewhere and worshipped. By their own account, they were uniquely happy in their marriage. Who knew but this was absolutely true?

Looking through a magazine at her hairdresser's, Julia read, *To deny love is the only crime.* The words were written in a box in the centre of the page. She read them again, liked them, remembered them, and introduced them to the company assembled for dinner the following night, thus furthering her reputation as a thinker.

Unluckily, a pedantic oaf called Edward Driscoll—who was *nothing*, yet seemed to consider himself *something*—had the crassness to put her statement on a different plane altogether.

'I wonder if that's true?' he said—as if it mattered—staring into his claret. 'Whoever said it would know what he meant, I suppose. He was probably right *then*, for himself. But generally, to deny love you must at some time have affirmed it. Surely, not to have done that would be a greater crime?

'Although,' he went on, incredibly, as if someone had contradicted him, 'if you like to say that no one should be held responsible for an inherent disability, you'd have a point.' He seemed to brood. Round about him, heads sank. 'Of course,' he glanced up quickly at Julia, 'he—that is, you—may have meant deny in that sense?'

Julia's eyes swivelled. Her mouth opened, then closed.

Driscoll resumed his monologue somewhat moodily. 'I suppose one is apt to blame people unfairly for blankness of feeling.'

Behind this lunatic's back, Ralph signalled to Julia: *What's he talking about?* She cast up her eyes.

'The trouble is,' Driscoll went on, 'there are people, and *people*, all looking very much like human beings.'

The smooth lid of Julia's left eye descended in a wink. It evoked five responsive smiles in the five who saw it.

'The total absence of empathy that you could assume in a cat in relation to a human being exists everywhere between people who are allegedly of one species,' Driscoll said. He wasn't bad-looking, either.

'And so what do you make of it all?' Julia asked

soothingly, with a tremendous bending of her personality over the young man.

He raised his eyes from the glass in his hand and smiled at Julia, obviously, disconcertingly, stone-cold sober.

'Maybe a new race of non-human people?' He seemed to consult her. 'Or the old race of non-humans increasing their numbers? Anyway, there are more and more of them all the time, and all disguised to look like humans.' His eyes were a striking sandy-gold colour.

In other circumstances, Julia felt she might have let rip, might have said something gigantically coarse and relieved her contempt. But she only said, 'Where are they coming from, do you think? Outer space?'

'Oh, yes.' He smiled. 'I should think so. Definitely.'

Inevitably, there were small failures in Julia's life but, as Ralph said, the tender-hearted ones of this world have always laid themselves open to failure, without ever letting it change them. If Julia had taken the Anne-Marie affair to heart, for instance, she wouldn't have been Julia.

Ralph and Julia were on the committee of an organisation dedicated to the relief of the needy. Through this charity they were brought into touch with Anne-Marie Grant, a neglected child of sixteen, the daughter of an alcoholic father, recently killed, and a mother, classified in the family's case history as 'weak and feckless', who had run off with a bus conductor to Melbourne after her husband's fatal accident.

Having decided to employ some young person to help the help in the house, Ralph and Julia interviewed and hired Anne-Marie for the job. As Julia put it to the girls, they fell in love with her on sight. She was beautiful. People who had only heard of girls with faces like flowers, seeing Anne-Marie, understood for the first time what the words meant and stopped to stare.

Moreover, as it appeared, she was sweet-natured, and innocent and quick to learn. Elsie adored her, and so did the cleaners, and Ralph and the boys.

If Anne-Marie had a fault, it was that she was a fraction cold and uncommunicative. Oh, she was intelligent, and even sensitive in a way, but there was a lack of heart somewhere in her that repelled Julia. Time and time again she failed to respond to Julia's sincere efforts to draw her out. And it wasn't—God knew—that Julia was prying. She only hoped the little soul would unburden herself of that dreadful past, shed as many tears as need be, and then take up her life like any normal girl.

'Don't worry, pet,' Ralph said. 'She'll come to you like all the others. She'll be your little disciple for life, wait and see.'

But, as the weeks continued to pass, the number of small wounding incidents began to mount. Anne-Marie took to avoiding Julia's eyes. She would not give smile for conspiratorial smile. Alternatively, she had a habit of looking at Julia out of those blue-grey eyes that were, in truth, like stars, and flowers, and precious stones. She looked at Julia with these wonderful eyes and seemed to think at her, or about her, in some disconcerting way.

Elsie did her share of damage by passing on to Julia one afternoon the details of a series of conversations *she* had had with Anne-Marie.

As hurt as she had ever been, indescribably bleak, Julia listened while painful revelations of deep feeling on the part of the child were repeated to *her*, by her own cook.

'Ah, she's had a hard time,' said Elsie. 'But I mustn't talk about that.'

It emerged that Anne-Marie saw herself as a nurse or a social worker like the one who'd rescued her. She wanted not to be left helpless and without skill in middle age, the way her mother had been. She wanted to learn all about the world, and not to marry till she was twenty-seven.

'She's seen too much of marriage to rush into it with maybe the wrong one,' the cook said sombrely.

'I said,' Julia later told Ralph drily, '"Look, don't encourage the girl's delusions of grandeur! She's had all of six years at school, so she isn't eligible to train as a dogcatcher! Do you know how many certificates girls have to have before they'll accept them as trainee nurses? That sort of future is *out* for Anne-Marie, and it's no kindness to her to pretend otherwise."'

'How soon people's lives are over and ruined!' cried Elsie.

Julia continued, quite brusquely for Julia, 'It's obvious she was made to settle down and have babies, anyway.' (If *Julia* had accepted this role as her destiny, was it too much to expect Anne-Marie to do the same?)

But Elsie could be stubborn. She pounded the bit of dough she was mangling about, showing that she meant to continue inciting the girl.

So Julia had no choice but to talk to Anne-Marie herself.

It took forty minutes and several cigarettes to put the matter of her future into perspective for the child. They were in Julia's lovely bedroom, a room coloured mother-of-pearl, with views of trees and lawns and sky. Anne-Marie looked down at her hands throughout, except when ordered to lift her head.

There was something forbidding about the girl's small Mediterranean face. As she noticed and debated this and, inconceivably, felt herself rebuked, a whim tickled Julia. It was just a whim, a silly little notion in a corner of her mind. Then, miraculously, everything was all at once reversed and Julia found that she was just a tiny little person in a corner of the notion. She was impelled to mention the facts of life.

Julia was devoutly frank. It seemed necessary to pass on all the curious customs and practices of a sexual nature that had ever been brought to her attention. Many men and women must have lived their lives without knowing all the facts she bestowed on Anne-Marie. But you can never know too much about anything. It was for the child's own protection. And she did look so surprised.

'My God, look at the time! Off you run, you baby Cleopatra! You've made me late for my appointment.' Julia laughed, admiring her, and Anne-Marie rose to go.

When she swayed, Julia laughed again and looked closely into the girl's face. She had the dulled look of one who had suffered a shock to the mind. She grasped the back of the chair for balance, her eyes closed, and Julia laughed yet again, indulgently. There was more than one way of skinning a cat, as the old saying went. And more than one way of deflowering a virgin, too. The child was glassy-eyed.

It was typical of a number of disappointments that Julia endured over the years that Anne-Marie should have wandered off shortly after this, leaving no word of thanks or explanation. Everyone was upset, but there was nothing to be done. Ralph was preparing for a short series of television interviews—an ordeal he detested, being a man of action rather than words—and Julia had to help him rehearse. Also the boys' school concert, *the* charity ball of the year, and one of her most lavish parties to date all fell in the same few days.

'Really, there's never a moment!' Julia said. What with marquees and floodlights in the garden to think about, and workmen tramping up and down the paths, and grouse, salmon, truffles, and pheasants being flown in from Europe for the occasion, and the disciples fleeing about on her behalf when they could escape from their tedious offices, it was impossible to give much thought to Anne-Marie's fate.

That ghastly Edward Driscoll sought her out at a diplomatic party to say, 'They've invented a death ray, Julia, to kill us all off.'

'Good on them!' she said, hostile. 'Who have?'

'The non-humans, remember? From outer space. They're highly organised.'

Julia humoured him. 'Why would they want to kill anyone? It's such a lovely night!'

'Well,' he said, almost apologetically, 'they *are* insane.' He seemed to know what Julia was thinking. 'It makes them dangerous.'

Julia cast into the depths. In the most condescending tone she had ever commanded in her life, she asked, 'Are you afraid of dying, Edward?'

'Yes,' he said.

With closed lips she smiled and turned away. If only she had had a death ray handy!

Kate (or Alice, or Brenda, or Valerie) spotted Anne-Marie in Hyde Park one day, a few months after she had left the house. She was pregnant, and her hands were ringless. Apparently she was in some bizarre get-up, with her hair straggling down her back, and looking miserable as sin.

Julia was terrifically interested when she heard. Looking as if she'd won a bet with herself, she started to laugh. 'Pregnant! Silly little thing! Why didn't she use something?'

Elsie cried and carried on when she heard the news, saying that the girl was capable of doing something desperate. 'Suicide, even!' Elsie cried. 'You didn't know her!'

Suicide! Some people had morbid minds.

No small failure ever changed Julia. She continued to lead the loveliest life. On Sundays, when they were free for a few hours, she and Ralph took the boys out sailing, or to watch polo matches. Ralph opened more branch offices. There were exhibitions of modern painting and pottery to arrange on behalf of Julia's pet charity, and talk of another royal visit to Australia. Edward Driscoll mysteriously vanished, and none of the disciples sighted Anne-Marie again. The world situation got worse, and then better, and then worse again. No one more remarkable than Julia ever appeared. No one took up the gauntlet she had thrown in the face of the universe.

7
The Beautiful Climate

The Shaws went down to the cottage on Scotland Island every weekend for two years. Hector Shaw bought the place from some hotelkeeper he knew, never having so much as hinted at his intention till the contract was signed. Then he announced to his wife and daughter the name of a certain house, his ownership of it, its location, and the fact that they would all go down every Friday night to put it in order.

It was about an hour's drive from Sydney. At the Church Point wharf they would park the car, lock it up, and wait for the ferry to take them across to the island.

Five or six families made a living locally, tinkering with boats and fishing, but most of the houses round about were weekenders, like the Shaws' place. Usually these cottages were sold complete with a strip of waterfront and a jetty. In the Shaws' case the jetty was a long spindly affair of grey wooden palings on rickety stilts, with a perpendicular ladder that had to be climbed getting in and out of the boat. Some of the others were handsome constructions equipped with special flags and lights to summon the ferryman when it was time to return to civilisation.

As Mr Shaw had foretold, they were constantly occupied putting the house in order, but now and then he would buy some green prawns, collect the lines from the spare-bedroom cupboard, and take his family into the middle of the bay to fish. While he made it obligatory to assume that this was a treat, he performed every action with his customary air of silent, smouldering violence, as if to punish misdemeanours, alarming his wife and daughter greatly.

Mrs Shaw put on her big straw sunhat, tied it solemnly under her chin, and went behind him down the seventy rough rock steps from the house. She said nothing. The glare from the water gave her a migraine. Since a day years before when she was a schoolgirl learning to swim and had almost drowned, she had had a horror of deep water. Her husband knew it. He was a difficult man, for what reason no one had been able to discover, least of all Hector Shaw himself.

Del followed her mother down the steep bushy track, not speaking, her nerves raw, her soundless protests battering the air about her. She did not *want* to go; nor, of course, could she stay when her absence would be used against her mother.

They were not free. Either the hostage, or the one over whom a hostage was held, they seemed destined to play forever if they meant to preserve the peace. And peace had to be preserved. Everything had always been subordinated to this task. As a child, Del had been taught that happiness was nothing but the absence of unpleasantness. For all she knew, it was true. Unpleasantness, she knew, could be extremely disagreeable. She knew that what was irrational had to be borne, and she knew she and her mother longed for peace and quiet—since she had been told so often. But still she did not want to go.

Yet that they should not accompany her father was unthinkable. That they should all three be clamped together was, in a way, the whole purpose of the thing. Though Del and her mother were aware that he might one day sink the boat deliberately. It wasn't *likely*, because he was terrified of death, whereas his wife would welcome oblivion, and his daughter had a stony capacity for endurance (so regarding death, at least, they had the upper hand); but it was *possible*. Just as he might crash the car some day on purpose if all three were secure together in it.

'Why do we *do* it?' Del asked her mother relentlessly. 'You'd think we were mental defectives, the way we troop behind him and do what we're told just to save any trouble. And it never does. Nothing we do makes sure of anything.

When I go out to work every day it's as if I'm out on parole. You'd think we were hypnotised.'

Her mother sighed and failed to look up, and continued to butter the scones.

'*You're* his wife, so maybe you think you have to do it, but I don't. I'm eighteen.'

However, till quite recently she had been a good deal younger, and most accustomed to being used in the cause of peace. Now her acquiescence gnawed at her and baffled her; but, though she made isolated stands, in essence she always did submit. Her few rebellions were carefully gauged to remain within the permitted limits, the complaints of a prisoner of war to the camp commandant.

This constant nagging from the girl exhausted Mrs Shaw. Exasperation penetrated even her alarming headaches. She asked desperately, 'What would you do if you *didn't* come? You're too nervous to stay in town by yourself. And if you did, what would you do?'

'*Here.* I have to come *here*, but why do we have to go in the boat?' On a lower note, Del muttered, 'I wish I worked at the kindergarten seven days a week; I dread the nights and weekends.'

She could *think* a thing like that, but never say it without a deep feeling of shame. Something about her situation made her feel not only, passively, abused, but actively, surprisingly, guilty.

All Del's analysis notwithstanding, the fishing expeditions took place whenever the man of the family signified his desire for some sport. Stationed in the dead centre of the glittering bay, within sight of their empty house, they sat in the open boat, grasping cork rollers, feeling minute and interesting tugs on their lines from time to time, losing bait, and catching three-inch fish.

Low hills densely covered with thin gums and scrub sloped down on all sides to the rocky shore. They formed silent walls of a dark subdued green, without shine. Occasional painted roofs showed through. Small boats puttered past and disappeared.

As the inevitable pain began to saturate Mrs Shaw's head, she turned gradually paler. She leaned against the side of the boat with her eyes closed, her hands obediently clasping the fishing line she had been told to hold.

The dazzle of the heavy summer sun sucked up colour till the scene looked black. Her light skin began to burn. The straw sunhat was like a neat little oven in which her hair, her head, and all its contents were being cooked.

Without expression, head lowered, Del looked at her hands, fingernails, legs, at the composition of the cork round which her line was rolled. She glanced sometimes at her mother, and sometimes, by accident, she caught sight of her father's bare feet or his arm flinging out a newly baited line, or angling some small silver fish off the hook and throwing it back, and her eyes sheered away.

The wooden interior of the boat was dry and burning. The three fishers were seared, beaten down by the sun. The bait smelled. The water lapped and twinkled blackly but could not be approached: sharks abounded in the bay.

The cottage was fairly dilapidated. The walls needed painting inside and out, and parts of the veranda at the front and both sides had to be re-floored. In the bedrooms, sitting room, and kitchen, most of the furniture was old and crudely made. They burned the worst of it, replacing it with new stuff, and what was worth salvaging Mrs Shaw and Del gradually scrubbed, sanded and painted.

Mr Shaw did carpentering jobs, and cleared the ground nearby of some of the thick growth of eucalyptus gums that had made the rooms dark. He installed a generator, too, so that they could have electric light instead of relying on kerosene lamps at night.

Now and then his mood changed inexplicably, for reasons so unconnected with events that no study and perpetuation of these external circumstances could ensure a similar result again. Nevertheless, knowing it could not last, believing it might, Mrs Shaw and Del responded shyly, then enthusiastically, but always with respect and circumspection, as if a friendly lion had come to tea.

These hours or days of amazing good humour were

passed, as it were, a few feet off the ground, in an atmosphere of slightly hysterical gaiety. They sang, pumping water to the tanks; they joked at either end of the saw, cutting logs for winter fires; they ran, jumped, slithered, and laughed till they had to lean against the trees for support. They reminded each other of all the incidents of other days like these, at other times when his nature was in eclipse.

'We'll fix up a nice shark-proof pool for ourselves,' he said. 'We own the water frontage. It's crazy not to be able to cool off when we come down. If you can't have a dip here, surrounded by water, what's the sense? We'd be better to stay home and go to the beach, in this weather.'

'Three cheers!' Del said. 'When do we start?'

The seasons changed. When the nights grew colder, Mr Shaw built huge log fires in the sitting room. If his mood permitted, these fires were the cause of his being teased, and he liked very much to be teased.

Charmed by his own idiosyncrasy, he would pile the wood higher and higher, so that the walls and ceiling shone and flickered with the flames, and the whole room crackled like a furnace on the point of explosion. Faces scorching, they would rush to throw open the windows, then they'd fling open the doors, dying for air. Soon the chairs nearest the fire would begin to smoke and then everyone would leap outside to the dark veranda, crimson and choking. Mr Shaw laughed and coughed till he was hoarse, wiping his eyes.

For the first few months, visitors were nonexistent, but one night on the ferry the Shaws struck up a friendship with some people called the Rivers, who had just bought a cottage next door. They came round one Saturday night to play poker and have supper, and in no time weekly visits to each other's house were established as routine. Grace and Jack Rivers were relaxed and entertaining company. Their easy good nature fascinated the Shaws, who looked forward to these meetings seriously, as if the Rivers were a sort of rest cure ordered by a specialist, from which they might pick up some health.

'It was too good to last,' Mrs Shaw said later. 'People are so funny.'

The Rivers' son, Martin, completed his army training and went down to stay on the island for a month before returning to his marine-engineering course at a technical college in town. He and Del met sometimes and talked, but she had not gone sailing with him when he asked her, nor was she tempted to walk across the island to visit his friends who had a pool.

'Why not?' he asked.

'Oh, well...' She looked down at the dusty garden from the veranda where they stood. 'I have to paint those chairs this afternoon.'

'*Have* to?' Martin had a young, open, slightly freckled face. Del looked at him, feeling old, not knowing how to explain how complicated it would be to extricate herself from the house, and her mother and father. He would never understand

the drama, the astonishment, that would accompany her statement to them. Even if, eventually, they said, 'Go, go!' recovering
from their shock, her own joylessness and fatigue were so clear
to her in anticipation that she had no desire even to test her
strength in the matter.

But one Saturday night, over a game of cards, Martin
asked her parents if he might take her the next night to a party
across the bay. A friend of his, Noel Stacey, had a birthday to
celebrate.

Del looked at him with mild surprise. He had asked her.
She had refused.

Her father laughed a lot at this request as though it were
very funny, or silly, or misguided, or simply impossible. It
turned out that it *was* impossible. They had to get back to
Sydney early on Sunday night.

If they *did* have to, it was unprecedented, and news to Del.
But she looked at her father with no surprise at all.

Martin said, 'Well, it'll be a good party,' and gave her a
quizzical grin. But his mother turned quite pink, and his father
cleared his throat gruffly several times. The game broke up a
little earlier than usual, and, as it happened, was the last one
they ever had together.

Not knowing that it was to be so, however, Mrs Shaw
was pleased that the matter had been dealt with so kindly
and firmly. 'What a funny boy!' she said later, a little coyly,
to Del.

'Is he?' she said indifferently.

'One of the new generation,' said Mr Shaw, shaking his head, and eyeing her with caution.

'Oh?' she said, and went to bed.

'She didn't really want to go to that party at all,' her mother said.

'No, but we won't have him over again, do you think? He's got his own friends. Let him stick to them. There's no need for this. These fellows who've been in army camps—I know what they're like.'

'She hardly looked at him. She didn't care.' Mrs Shaw collected the six pale-blue cups, saucers, and plates on the wooden tray, together with the remnants of supper.

With his back to the fire, hands clasped behind him, Mr Shaw brooded. 'He had a nerve, though, when you come to think of it. I mean—he's a complete stranger.'

Mrs Shaw sighed anxiously, and her eyes went from one side of the room to the other. 'I'm sure she didn't like him. She doesn't take much interest in boys. You're the only one.'

Mr Shaw laughed reluctantly, looking down at his shoes.

As more and more of the property was duly painted and repaired, the Shaws tended to stop work earlier in the day, perhaps with the unspoken intention of making the remaining tasks last longer. Anyway, the pressure was off, and Mrs Shaw knitted sweaters, and her husband played patience, while

Del was invariably glued to some book or other.

No one in the district could remember the original owner-builder of their cottage, or what he was like. But whether it was this first man, or a later owner, someone had left a surprisingly good library behind. It seemed likely that the builder had lived and died there, and that his collection had simply been passed on with the property from buyer to buyer, over the years.

Books seemed peculiarly irrelevant on this remote hillside smelling of damp earth and wood smoke and gums. The island had an ancient, prehistoric, undiscovered air. The alphabet had yet to be invented.

However, the books *had* been transported here by someone, and Del was pleased to find them, particularly the many leather-bound volumes of verse. Normally, in an effort to find out why people were so peculiar, she read nothing but psychology. Even after she knew psychologists did not know, she kept reading it from force of habit, in the hope that she might come across a formula for survival directed specifically at her: *Del Shaw, follow these instructions to the letter!* Poetry was a change.

She lay in a deckchair on the deserted side veranda and read in the mellow three o'clock, four o'clock sunshine. There was, eternally, the smell of grass and burning bush, and the homely noise of dishes floating up from someone's kitchen along the path of yellow earth, hidden by trees. And she hated the chair, the mould-spotted book, the sun, the smells, the sounds, her supine self.

They came unto a land in which it seemed always afternoon.

'It's like us, exactly like us and this place,' she said to her mother, fiercely brushing her long brown hair in front of the dressing table's wavy mirror. 'Always afternoon. Everyone lolling about. Nobody *doing* anything.'

'My goodness!' Her mother stripped the sheets off the bed to take home to the laundry. 'I thought we'd all been active enough this weekend to please anyone. And I don't see much afternoon about Monday morning.'

'Active! That isn't what I mean. Anyway, I don't mean here or this weekend. I mean everyone, everywhere, all the time. Ambling round till they die.' Oh, but that wasn't what she meant, either.

Mrs Shaw's headache look appeared. 'It's off to the doctor with you tonight, miss!'

Del set her teeth together. When her mother had left the room with her arms full of linen, still darting sharp glances at her daughter, Del closed her eyes and raised her face to the ceiling.

Let me *die*.

The words seemed to be ground from her voiceless body, to be ground, powdered stone, from her heart.

She breathed very slowly; she slowly righted her head, carefully balancing its weight on her neck. Then she pulled on her suede jacket, lifted her bag, and clattered down the uneven stone steps to the jetty. It always swayed when anyone set foot on it.

When the cottage had been so patched and cleaned that, short of a great expenditure of capital, no further improvement was possible, Hector Shaw ceased to find any purpose in his visits to it. True, there was still the pool to be tackled, but the summer had gone by without any active persuasion, any pleading, any teasing, from his wife and daughter. And if *they* were indifferent, far be it from him...

Then there was another thing. Not that it had any connection with the place, with being on Scotland Island, but it had the side effect of making the island seem less—safe, salubrious, desirable. Jack Rivers died from a heart attack one Sunday morning. Only fifty-five he was, and a healthier-looking fellow you couldn't have wished to meet.

Since the night young Martin Rivers had ruined their poker parties, they had seen very little of Jack and Grace. Sometimes on the ferry they had bumped into each other, and when they had the Shaws, at least, were sorry it had all worked out so badly. Jack and Grace were good company. It was hard not to feel bitter about the boy having spoiled their nice neighbourly friendship so soon before his father died. Perhaps if Jack had spent more time playing poker and less doing whatever he did do after the Saturdays stopped...

On a mild midwinter night, a few weeks after Jack Rivers' funeral, the Shaw family sat by the fire. Del was gazing along her corduroy slacks into the flames, away from her book. Her parents were silent over a game of cards.

Mr Shaw took a handful of cashew nuts from a glass dish at his side and started to chew. Then, leaning back in his chair, his eyes still fixed on his cards, he said, 'By the way, the place's up for sale.'

His wife stared at him. 'What place?'

'*This* place.' He gave her his sour, patient look. 'It's been on Dalgety's books for three weeks.'

'What for?' Del asked, conveying by the gentleness of her tone her total absence of criticism. It was dangerous to question him, but then it was dangerous not to, too.

'Well, there isn't much to do round here now. And old Jack's popped off—' (He hadn't meant to say that!) Crunching the cashew nuts, he slid down in his chair expansively, every supra-casual movement premeditated as though he were playing Hamlet at Stratford.

The women breathed deeply, not without regret, merely accepting this new fact in their lives. Mrs Shaw said, 'Oh!' and Del nodded her comprehension. Changing their positions imperceptibly, they prepared to take up their occupations again in the most natural and least offensive ways they could conceive. There was enormous potential danger in any radical change of this sort.

'Ye—es,' said Mr Shaw, drawing the small word out to an extraordinary length. 'Dalgety's telling them all to come any Saturday or Sunday afternoon.' Still he gazed at his handful of cards, then he laid them face down on the table, and with a thumb thoughtfully rubbed the salt from the cashews into the palm of his other hand. It crumbled onto his knees, and he dusted it down to the rug, seeming agreeably occupied in its distribution.

'Ye—es,' he said again, while his wife and daughter gazed at him painfully. 'When and if anyone takes the place, I think we'd better use the cash to go for a trip overseas. What do you say? See the Old Country…Even the boat trip's pretty good, they tell me. You go right round the coast here (that takes about a week), then up to Colombo, Bombay, Aden, through the Suez, then up through the Mediterranean, through the Straits of Messina past some volcano, and past Gibraltar to Marseilles, then London.'

There was silence.

Mr Shaw turned away from the table and his game, and looked straight into his wife's grey eyes—a thing he rarely did. Strangers were all right, he could look at them, but with relations, old acquaintances, his spirit, unconscious, was ashamed and uneasy.

'Go away?' his wife repeated, turning a dreadful colour.

He said, 'Life's short. I've earned a holiday. Most of my typists've been abroad. We'll have a year. We'll need a year.

If someone turns up on the ferry one day and *wants* the place, that is. There's a bit of a slump in real estate just now, but I guess we'll be okay.'

And they looked at each other, the three of them, with unfamiliar awe. They were about to leave this dull pretty city where they were all so hard to live with, and go to places they had read about, where the world was, where things happened, where the photographs of famous people came from, where history was, and snow in cities, and works of art, and splendour…

Poetry and patience were discarded from that night, while everyone did extra jobs about the cottage to add to its attractiveness and value. Mrs Shaw and Del planted tea trees and hibiscus bushes covered with flowers of palest apricot, and pink streaked with red. Mr Shaw cemented the open space under the house (it was propped up on columns on its steep hillside) and the area underneath was like a large extra room, shady and cool. They put some long bamboo chairs down there, fitted with cushions.

Most weekend afternoons, jobs notwithstanding, Del went to the side veranda to lean over the railing out of sight and watch the ferry go from jetty to jetty and return to Church Point. She watched and willed, but no one ever came to see the house.

It was summer again, and the heatwave broke records. Soon it was six months since the night they had talked about the trip.

Always the island was the same. It was scented, self-sufficient; the earth was warm underfoot, and the air warm to breathe. The hillside sat there, quietly, rustling quietly, a smug curving hillside that had existed for a long time. The water was blue and sparkled with meaningless beauty. Smoke stood in the sunny sky above the bush here and there across the bay, where other weekend visitors were cooking chops, or making coffee on fuel stoves.

Del watched the ferries and bargained with fate, denying herself small pleasures, which was easy for her to do. She waited. Ferries came and went round the point, but never called at their place.

They lost heart. In the end, it would have been impossible even to mention the trip. But they all grieved with a secret enduring grief, as if at the death of the one person they had loved. Indeed, they grieved for their own deaths. Each so unknown and un-understood, who else could feel the right regret? From being eaten by the hillside, from eating one another, there had been the chance of a reprieve. Now it was evidently cancelled, and in the meantime irretrievable admissions had been made.

At the kindergarten one Tuesday afternoon Miss Lewis, who was in charge, called Del to the telephone. She sat down, leaning her forehead on her hand before lifting the receiver.

'Hello?'

'Del, your father's sold the cottage to a pilot. Somebody

Davies. He's bought the tickets. We've just been in to get our cabins. We're leaving in two months.'

'What? A pilot?'

'Yes. We're going on the *Arcadia* on the 28th of November. The cabins are lovely. Ours has got a porthole. We'll have to go shopping, and get injections and passports…'

'We're *going*?'

'Of course we are, you funny girl! We'll tell you all about it when you get home tonight. I've started making lists.'

They were going. She was going away. Out in the world she would escape from them. There would be room to run, outside this prison.

'So, we're off,' her mother said.

Del leaned sideways against the wall, looking out at the eternal afternoon, shining with all its homey peace and glory. 'Oh, that's good,' she said. 'That's good.'

8
Lance Harper, His Story

What's a classic? Lance Harper wondered. He was sitting in a bar watching television the night he wondered this for exactly the millionth time. And, surely, with the millionth assault on this intractable question, Lance's feeling for it could be said to have passed from passion to monomania. If so, it could account for what happened.

Sometimes he used to say to his mother, 'I don't know why I'm living, Mum.' And she, hearing that he was no more than half-joking, was proud that Lance was not like other boys, and did not even think, You were an accident, Lance.

But he mightn't have cared, anyway. What is a classic? That was the point. He had hoped, when the whole question of classics presented itself to him, that as he was going on twenty-one, five feet eleven and still growing, his last wisdom tooth almost through, the answer was an instinctive thing like all the rest, and one morning he would wake up knowing. But he hadn't.

Now, anyone observant could have seen he wasn't well: he seldom smiled, his naturally deep-set, dark-grey eyes receded, melancholy, under his brow. But, of course, one of the facts of Lance's life was that it had never contained a soul who had dreamed of observing him. And his heavy frame, hollowed out by restless days and listless nights, looked healthy enough as he swung along the girders of each new skyscraper.

'He's a fabulous colour,' his mother, Pearl, told her boss, running up another red Christmas stocking on the machine. 'Fabulous tan. And his hair's all yellow with the sun.'

'Got a girl?' Bert measured off red cloth.

'No. His mum's the only girl Lance's interested in.'

Bert paused and looked at her.

'That's all right! You can scoff! He's working overtime to pay off a new fridge for me, and he's trading in his car for a new one so I can be comfortable when we go out.'

'I'll get some more of that cotton,' said Bert, disappearing.

So that close, hostile look of perplexity on Lance's face was never remarked. It was his habitual way of looking and was mistaken for the quizzical squint the sun gives most Australian men. Lance's dad had it, too, but with him it really was the sun.

He was a builder by trade, like Lance, and swarmed over scaffolding in all weathers.

When Lance was five his mother went away one night without him, just stopping to hiss in his dark room, 'Yes, I'm going, love. Dad's sending me away. He says you both like Myrna Barnes better than Mum. What? You don't? Well, someone's telling lies to poor old Mum. I'm off, anyway, Lance. Do what Mrs Barnes tells you.'

And his father said, 'What? Where's she gone? What? I'll give you a good clip on the ear if I hear any more out of you. Get out into the back yard! Go on!'

About once a year after that, his mum or dad left home forever. The period of absence varied, and sometimes Lance was taken, sometimes kept, but the departures were fairly predictable and made quite a stable feature in his life.

He was invariably placed on one side of the dispute as if by some impartial referee: now he was Dad's boy, now Mum's. But sometimes, in odd moments of reconciliation, it struck his parents that Lance was a boy who kept things up too long—a moody boy, nice-looking but not nice. And sometimes they combined to chide him for his lack of friends. Not that *they* had any friends, but occasionally they felt it would be normal and flattering to them if Lance would extend himself and acquire a few.

If he did not approve of them, let him be better!

But Lance took up no challenges. His mind seemed always

to be, whatever the subject in front of him, deeply concentrated on something else. He was never at a loss for thought. In the house there was always something to set his mind turning: egg stuck to the ceiling where plates of breakfast had been hurled; scars on Mum's hands where she was burned while wrestling with Dad and a pot of beans in boiling water; the scar above his own right eyebrow where an ashtray had hit him once; a broken record player; a slashed bike tyre.

Pearl was away when Lance had his fifteenth birthday and started work. In due course she brought home her circled eyes, her case full of shocking-pink nighties and underwear, and found a new vacuum cleaner from Lance tied up in cellophane in the hall, and a bottle of French perfume on her oak dressing table. And that was only the beginning. She had had no idea Lance was so fond of her. He gave presents to his father, too, at first—tools and fishing gear and shaving kits. What a generous boy!

As a family the Harpers had often been hard up. It wasn't simple to pay off the television set, piano, two transistor radios, a Model Homes electric stove, two electric shavers, a portable typewriter, a car, and furniture, all at once. But Lance worked overtime, and paid his mother more than amply for his bed and food. He was a real help. She took a new notion to him.

(Their house was a wooden one and quite old, but not set in deep suburbia. The rent was small; it was close to the city and, really, very snug.)

Once, when he was on night shift and supposed to be
sleeping by day in the empty house, Lance went to town and
came back with a large dictionary. Looking up every second
word—words like 'polemic' and 'rapprochement'—he read
from cover to cover a serious-looking political weekly from
London. He'd heard students talking about it one day at a
railway station bookstall. It was in English. He could not,
naturally, locate definitions of cartoons or the groups signified
by initials alone, but at first he did find all the other words. It
was the best dictionary in the biggest bookshop in Sydney.

Apart from what he made out to be political stuff by the
way the names of the countries kept turning up, Lance saw that
the weekly covered such topics as: Correspondence, the Arts
and Entertainment, Books, Reviews, Food and Wine, and
Positions Vacant. To begin with, chewing hard on a wooden
tooth cleaner (he didn't smoke), Lance looked up most of the
words in these sections, too. He also made a pot of coffee and
drank more than he wanted.

But the definitions often turned out to be as arid and
abstruse as the original terms, and Lance was obliged to
penetrate so far in search of the truth of each word, chasing it
through all the brand-new pages, that he began to flag at the
thought of the return journey to the text. There was a loss of
heart somewhere in the room, or in the weather, and Lance
glanced over his shoulder at the sky. 'I'm getting fed up with
this,' he said aloud.

Let it be understood that Lance wasn't stupid! Ages ago in infants' school he had often been top, or near the top, of his class, without trying. Even in high school, in second year, which was as far as he went, he alone of all the forty in the room had solved a certain, very difficult, problem in algebra one day. Think of that! Lance often did.

For several hours now he linked meaning to meaning, rewriting pages of the ninepenny weekly. Then he chewed another stick of medicated wood and read his reconstruction. This was in English, too.

He couldn't understand a single sentence.

And, finally, he had to admit that it was all, all of it, even the vacant jobs, joined to a past, a present, to people, places, and things, that he was more ignorant of than the man in the moon. He was old enough to fight and die in a war at this time.

One evening, not long afterwards, having in the meantime abandoned the dictionary in a bus, Lance was watching television, eating an apple, and painting his toenails with his mother's clear polish. The bottle happened to be on the arm of the chair he'd fallen into. Also, it was partly because (leaving aside his abstraction) he was wearing on his feet those plastic sandals, presumably modelled on Mercury's, that disfigured thousands of Sydney feet that summer, and which were called, without much splitting of hairs, thongs, tongs, or prongs, according to the mood of the speaker. But the point is that they left Lance's toenails bare, which was why he painted them when the lecturer talked on television about classics.

Lance came in at the tail end of this programme, just as the man said, 'Now for the summing-up.' He listened quite idly at first, but it would be no exaggeration to say that afterwards Lance was a man possessed. The speaker had really smouldered with conviction, using all his force to prove that a man who knew his classics knew everything worth knowing.

'Good heavens, Lance, don't let your father catch you with paint on your toenails!'

Lance said, 'I never noticed,' and went to his room with cotton wool and polish remover. In fact, though, he and his father hadn't spoken a word to each other in eighteen months. It wasn't likely his feet would have started them talking.

In a clean white shirt, in a new tie and suit, Lance set out for an evening class advertised in Saturday's big paper along with movies and nightclubs—the first of a course of ten lectures. He had a mushroom omelette in a restaurant near the lecture hall, and his hand shook when he stirred his coffee. It was a pity he didn't smoke.

When he looked at his watch, a man with a briefcase sat down opposite. Lance felt his mind drop suddenly, glide, fall, and swoop back to position. He said, 'You're Harold Jefferson. I saw you on TV.'

Harold Jefferson looked up. He was a remarkably handsome man and good at his job. 'Yes, I did give a talk recently.'

Then he ordered a meal and took some papers from his briefcase, not glancing up again, his equable spirit quivering at the echo of that bald address, the mental picture of that watch and suit, so spruce and naïve, and, above all, at that look in the brilliant deep-set eyes of the fellow across the table. It had been an immensely stupid look of something like veneration—because *he* was a television 'personality'!

'I'd like to ask you something, if you don't mind.'

Oh, really! Harold thought. He was a nervous man of kindly instincts, but his most natural instinct now was to jump heavily on whoever it was prostrated before him. This silly character (probably some would-be Elvis Presley hoping for television contacts) was humble, honoured *him*, Harold Jefferson, and for the wrong reasons! How despicable it made him seem!

'If *you* don't mind,' he murmured, not looking up. 'I'm lecturing tonight.' Harold did have charm, but he did like to discriminate a little in its use.

'Yes, I know. I'm going to be there. Mr Jefferson, you talked about the classics. You said they could make a man free, and sort of rich in himself. I liked that. I never heard anything like it before.'

Harold had to smile with pleasure and shame. He couldn't help but feel himself to be the charmed one now. These rough diamonds! You read about them and dismissed them, but they did have a certain ingenuous something.

He said, 'I'm glad you liked it,' and allowed himself the licence of comparing their probable backgrounds: there was no doubt that that fellow's would be the richer materially. Harold had gone from a Midlands town to Oxford on a government grant. In *this* fellow's background he divined quite easily (couldn't he see a more expensive suit than he had ever owned?) the latest car, the typewriter no one could use, the piano no one could play and, probably, he thought, a large dog no one exercised.

Lance said, 'What's a classic?' And Harold grew pink, and got pinker, though his expression didn't alter. He'd been made a fool of! Either he was chatting with an imbecile or he was being taken for a fool! Probably because he was English.

But no, he realised slowly. This poor chap was genuine, all right. What a pity! But even so!

Against his will, Harold started to smile. He had been working hard, correcting examination papers, preparing lectures, trying to persuade a girl in London to come out and marry him. He was tired. He simply had to laugh.

Lance went to earth like someone mortally wounded. He put down some money and walked out into the street towards the nearest bar.

Still laughing, but half-rising in alarm to restrain him, Harold Jefferson called his apologies, dropped his briefcase, stooped to collect his papers, and lost his man.

*

'Mum, I've signed on to a ship. I'm leaving on Friday. I'm going to the States on Friday.'

'What? Leaving me, son? You're all I've got, Lance, love.'

'*He's* still here. And I've got you a big dog so you won't be lonely.'

'A dog? How'll I feed it, Lance?'

'I don't know, Mum—with meat, I guess. I'll send you money.'

'I don't want a dog. I want you! You're all I've got.'

'No, I'm not, Mum. You'll like a dog.'

Pearl had shut herself away to cry for several hours. Lance didn't change his mind, though.

Across America he picked fruit and hiked and found odd jobs. In England, a man in a Chelsea pub said two words to him he would never forget: 'juxtapose' and 'machinations'. Lance often remembered the talk they had.

He spent quite a lot of time with women, and went quite off his mother. I'm all she's got *now*, he used to think. But he went home after two years, arriving around Christmas time. He took his mother Scotch woollies and things, forgetting the Sydney climate in December. The temperature was about a hundred and four in the shade. But Pearl was more than happy, sobbing half the day, and showing him off to the neighbours at night. The dog had got lost. His father was in hospital.

These days Lance drank more than he used to, and talked more, too. His mother thought this a big improvement. Her

Lance was fascinating, in a way. The way he said, for instance (so peculiar, really, she couldn't think what he meant), 'No one could tell me what a classic is, Mum. I asked them all.'

'A classic, love? I didn't know you wanted to know.'

'Of course I did! Of course I did!' She seemed so silly to him, he thought she must be drunk. His own mother! Never mind!

That night he wandered the Sydney streets, and wound up in a bar watching television. It was here he asked his question for the millionth time. Afterwards, though he went over and over the scene in his mind, he could never be sure of his reason for throwing a bottle through the screen, and all the rest...

Lance got three months for this effort, and a further three later on, for assaulting a guard. That sounds worse, that last bit, than it really was. Lance and the guard were friendly; it turned out they'd both sailed on the same ship at one time, so the assault was no more than the token push they'd agreed on.

As buildings go in Australia, the prison was ancient, and none too comfortable, but it was redeemed in Lance's eyes, at least, as anyone will believe, by the fact that an eccentric, now deceased, clerk had bequeathed his vast collection of books, as his will phrased it, 'to those unfortunates incarcerated behind stone walls'.

On the second night of his imprisonment Lance discovered

in the library shelf upon shelf of a series called *All the Classics* and, accompanying the series, several copies of *The Plain Man's Guide to the Understanding and Appreciation of All the Classics*.

This useful book is now said to be, unhappily, out of print.

9
The Cost of Things

Dan Freeman shut the white-painted garage doors and went across the paved courtyard to the house, which was painted a glossy white, too. *A lovely home.* Visitors always used these words to describe it, and Dan always looked intent and curious when they did, as if he suspected them of irony. But the house did impress him, for all that he wasn't fond of it.

When the Freemans bought the place they said apologetically to their friends that they couldn't afford it, *but...* People just looked unfriendly and didn't smile back. Then came the grind, the worry, fear, boredom, paring down, the sacrifices large and small of material and, it really did seem, spiritual comforts, the eternal use of the negative, habitual meanness, harassment. And it wasn't paid for yet, not *yet*. They had been careful, he and Mary, though, to see that the children hadn't—to use Mary's phrase—gone without.

Lately, Dan had begun to think it mightn't have done any harm if Bill and Laura *had* been a bit deprived. They might now be applying themselves to their books occasionally, and thinking about scholarships. But, oh no! They had no doubt their requirements would be all supplied just for the wanting. Marvellous! The amount of work they did, it would be a miracle if either of them matriculated.

'Hello. You're late. Dinner's ready,' Mary called as the back door closed.

Leaning round into the kitchen, he looked at her seriously and sniffed the air. 'What is it?'

'Iced soup. Your special steak. Salad with—'

He rolled his eyes. 'There's the paper. Five minutes to get cleaned up and I'm with you.'

Mary was an excellent cook. The Freemans had always eaten well, but since Dan had come home from his six months' interstate transfer she had outdone herself. 'I experimented while you were away,' she explained, producing dinners nightly that would have earned their house several stars in the *Guide Michelin* had it ever been examined in this light.

'Experimented!' Dan laughed in an unreal, very nearly guilty, way the first time she said this, because he was listening to another voice in his head reply smartly, So did I! So did I!

Feeling the way he felt or, rather, remembering the name

Clea, he was shocked at the gleeful fellow in him who could treat that name simply as something secret from Mary. And he thought, I am ashamed, although he did not *feel* ashamed to find himself taking pride in the sombre and splendid addition to his past that the name represented. Clea, he thought, as if it were some expensive collector's item he had picked up, not without personal risk, for which it was not unnatural to accept credit. At the sound of that guilty laugh or the puffing of vanity, Dan mentally groaned and muttered, 'I'm sorry. I'm sorry.'

For the first weeks after his return to Melbourne he had blocked all memories of those Sydney months, since he could not guarantee the behaviour of his mind; and if to remember in such ways was to dishonour, he had emerged out of a state of careful non-consideration with the impression that to remember truly might not be wise. But lately, lately…He had realised that lately when he was alone he sat for hours visualising his own hand reaching to grasp hers. And each time he produced this scene its significance had to be considered afresh, without words, through timeless periods of silence. Or he pictured her walking away from him as he had once seen her do. An occasion of no significance at all. She had merely been a few steps in front of him. And he pictured her arms rising. For hours, weeks, he had watched her walk away. Then for nights, days, and weeks he had looked at the movement of her arms.

He could not see her face.

Wrenching his mind back with all his energy and concentration, he set about tracking down her face, methodically collecting her features and firmly assembling them. The results were static portraits of no one in particular, faded and distant as cathedral paintings of angels and martyrs. These faces were curiously, painfully undisturbing, as meaningless as the dots on a radar screen to an untrained observer.

In their elaborate dining room he and Mary sat at the long table dipping spoons into chilled soup.

'Where are the kids?'

'Bill's playing squash with Philip, and Laura's over at Rachel's. They're all going on to a birthday party together.'

'At this time of night?'

'They have to go through some records.'

'What about their work? I thought they agreed to put in three hours a night till the end of term?'

'You can't keep them home from a party, Dan. All the others are going.'

'All the others don't want to be physicists! Or they've got wealthy fathers and don't have to win scholarships. These two'll end up in a factory if they're not careful.'

Mary looked at him. 'You *are* in a bad mood. Did something go wrong at the office?'

'They're irresponsible. If they knew what a depression was like, or a war—'

'Now, don't spoil your dinner. How do you like the soup? At the last minute I discovered I didn't have any parsley and I had to use mint. What do you think? Is it awful?'

She hadn't altered her hairstyle since they were married. She still chose dresses that would have suited her when she was twenty and wore size ten. Her face was bare of make-up except for a rim of lipstick round the edge of her mouth. And there was something in the total of all this indifference that amounted to a crime.

How easily she had divested herself of the girl with the interests and pleasant ways. And what contempt she had felt for him and shown him, for having been so easily deceived, when she was sure of her home, her children. She had transformed herself before his eyes, laughing.

Anyway, he gave in when she wanted this house, which was pretentious and impossible for them, really. But he even thought he might find it a sort of hobby, a bulwark, himself. You have to have something.

'What are you looking at? Dan? Is it the mint? Is it awful?' She was really anxious. He lifted another spoonful from his plate and tasted it. Mary waited. He felt he ought to say something. 'Mary…' What had they been discussing?

'It's—extra good,' he said suddenly. '*Extra* good.'

She gave a little scoffing laugh. 'You sound like Bill.'

Not raising his eyes, he asked, 'What sort of a day have you had?' and Mary began to tell him while the creamy soup slid weirdly down his throat, seeming to freeze him to the marrow. He shivered. It was a warm summer night. Crickets were creaking in the garden outside.

'—and Bill wants to start golf soon. He asked me to sound you out about a set of clubs. And while I'm at it, Laura's hinting she'd like that French course on records. She says it'd be a help with the accent.'

'*Mary*,' he protested bitterly and paused, forgetting. 'For God's sake!' he added on the strength of his remembered feeling, gaining time. Then again, as before, the weight descended—the facts he knew, the emotions. 'What are you trying to do? You encourage them to want—impossible things. Why? To turn me into a villain when I refuse? You know how we stand. Your attitude baffles me.'

Mary's expression was rather blank but also rather triumphant.

He went on, and stammered slightly, 'I want them to have—everything. I grudge them nothing. But these grown-up toys—it can't be done. If Laura would stay home and work at her French—and Bill already has so many strings to his bow he can't hold a sensible conversation about anything. They'll end up bus conductors if they're not careful.'

Mary looked at him sharply. 'Have you been drinking, Dan?'

'Two beers.'

'I thought so! Really, if I have to hear you complain about

the cost of their education for the next six years, I don't think it would be worth it. Not to them either, I'm sure.'

He said nothing.

'*We* aren't going without anything. We've got the house and car. And the garden at weekends. It isn't as if we were young.' Mary waved an arm. 'But if you feel like this, ask them to repay you when they've qualified. They won't want to be indebted to you.'

He stared at her heavily, lifted his formal-looking squarish face with its blue eyes and stared at her, saying nothing. Mary breathed through her nose at him, then collected his plate and hers and went away to the kitchen.

'Clea…' It was a groan. Tears came to his eyes. It was the night he had thought to go away with her. They could *not* be parted. How could he explain? It was against nature, could not *be*. He would sell everything, and leave all but a small essential amount with Mary and the children. Then he and Clea would go—far away. And great liners trailing music and streamers sailed from Sydney daily for all the world's ports. Now that he'd found Clea, he would find the circumstances he had always expected, with their tests that would ask more of him than perseverance, resignation. They would live—somewhere, and be—very happy.

Common sense had cabled him at this point: this would all be quite charming, except for one minor problem that springs to mind.

What would they live on? A glorified clerk, his sole value as a worker lay in his memory of a thousand details relating to television films bought by the corporation. Away from the department he had no special knowledge, no money-raising skills. Could he begin to acquire a profession at forty-five? Living on what, in the meantime?

'There. At least there's nothing wrong with the steak.'

Mary looked at him expectantly, and he looked at the platter of food for some seconds. 'It's—done to a turn.'

'*Over*done?'

'No.' He thought of saying to her pleased face: I thought of deserting you, Mary. And he had, oh, he had. 'What? Yes, everything's fine.' The only trouble was that unfortunately, unfortunately, he was beginning to feel sick.

'Dan, I forgot to mention this since you got back. You're never here with all this extra work—'

'Yes?' Here it came: the proof that he had been right to return, that he and Mary *did* have a life in common. How often had he pleaded with Clea in those last days, 'You can't walk out on twenty years of memories.' (Not that she had ever asked or expected him to.)

'It's the roof. The tiles. There was a landslide into the azaleas while you were away. I thought you'd notice the broken bushes.'

'Oh.'

'So, do you think I should get someone to look over

the whole roof?'

'Yes, I suppose so.'

'Well, it's important to get it fixed before we start springing leaks.'

'Yes. All right. Ring Harvey. Get him to give us an estimate.'

'Dan? Where are you going? You haven't touched your dinner!'

'I'm sorry. I've got to get some air. No, stay there. Eat your dinner.'

'Aren't you well?' She half-rose from her chair, but he warded her off and compelled her to sink back to the table with a large forbidding movement of his arm. Mary shrugged, gave a tiny snort of boredom and disdain, and resumed eating.

Sydney…At the end of a week he had begun to look forward to getting back to Mary's cooking. The department wasn't lavish with away-from-home expenses for officers on his grade, and he had the usual accounts flying in from Melbourne by every post, in addition to an exorbitant hotel bill for the very ordinary room he occupied near the office. The hotel served a continental breakfast and no other meals. At lunchtime he and Alan Parker leapt out for beer and a sandwich which cost next to nothing, then by six o'clock he was famished. Somehow, surreptitiously, he started to treat himself to substantial and well-cooked dinners in restaurants all over the city. In Melbourne he only patronised places like these once a year, for a birthday or anniversary. He felt rather ill at ease eating, so to speak, Mary's new dress or the children's holidays, and he was putting on flesh. But—everything was hopeless. You had to have something. Yet money harassed him. He felt a kind of anguished dullness at the thought of it. It made him dwell on the place where it was cheaper and less worrying to be: home.

As the representative of his department, he was invited one Friday evening to an official cocktail party. A woman entered the building as he did, and together they ran for the row of automatic lifts, entered one, and were shot up to some height between the fourth and fifth floors and imprisoned there for over half an hour. Clea.

Dan's first thought was that she looked a bit flashy. Everything about her looked a fraction more colourful than was quite seemly: the peacock-blue dress, the blonde hair— not natural, the make-up and, in another sense, the drawling low-pitched voice. (This would certainly have been Mary's view.)

Then, while the alarm bell rang and caretakers and electricians shouted instructions at one another, they stood exchanging words and Dan looked into her eyes with the usual polite, rather stuffy, slightly patronising expression.

He was surprised. Under gold-painted lids, her blue eyes glanced up and actually saw him, with a look that twenty years, fifteen years, ago he had met daily in his mirror. It was as familiar as that. She wasn't *young*. It wasn't a young look. It was alarmingly straight. It was the look by which he had once identified his friends.

At the party when they were finally released, however, Clea treated him with wonderful reserve, recognising nothing about him. She remained steadfastly with the group least likely to succeed in charming the person Dan imagined her to be, smiling a lazy gallant smile, bestowing gestures and phrases on their sturdy sense. Showing pretty teeth, laughing huskily, she stood near them and *was*. When Dan approached, though, that all appeared to have been illusory. She was merely quiet, watchful, sceptical, an onlooker.

Ah, well! He put her from him. He expected nothing. It had been a momentary interest, and this wasn't the first time, after all, that circumstances had separated him from someone whom he would in some sense always know.

But he met her one day in the street accidentally. (Though Sydney is two million strong, people who live there can never lose touch, eager though they might be to do so.) He remembered they said something about the party, and something else about the lift, and then they said goodbye and parted. It wasn't till he had gone some eight or nine steps that Dan realised he had walked backwards from her.

The following Saturday night they met at another interdepartmental party and after that there were no backward steps till this inevitable, irrevocable return to hearth and home.

Clea had a flat—kitchen, bathroom, bedsitting room—in a converted harbourside mansion, and a minor executive job with a film unit that paid rent and food and clothing bills. Once she had been an art student, but at the end of four years she stopped attending classes and took a job.

'You were too critical of yourself,' Dan said. 'Your standards were too high.'

She smiled.

In her spare time she had continued to paint, she told Dan, and he had an impression of fierceness and energy, and he felt he knew how she must have looked. So she had painted. And it was why she was sane. And why people who knew nothing whatever about her liked to be near her. But ages ago, and permanently, she had laid it aside. That is, laid aside the doing, but not the looking, not the thinking, not finally herself.

Dan insisted on being shown the few pieces of work that she hadn't destroyed, and he examined them solemnly, and felt this discarded talent of Clea's was a thing to respect. In addition (and less respectably, he knew), he saw it as a decoration of her personality not unflattering to himself. From talk of art, which he invariably started, he would find he had led the way back to that perennially sustaining subject—their first meeting.

'At the party that night, why were you so—cold?'

'For good reasons. Which you know. How many times do you think I can survive this sort of thing?'

They were in Clea's room on an old blue sofa by the fire. Dan turned his head away, saying nothing. She said, 'It's no fun. You get tired. Like a bird on the wing, and no land. It's—no fun. You feel trapped and hunted at the same time. And the weather seems menacing. (No, I don't mean now. But there have been times.) And in the long run it's so much less effort to stay where your belongings are…Wives shouldn't worry too much. And even other women shouldn't. By the time they find themselves listening to remorseful remembrances of things past they're too—killed to care. And they find they can prompt their loved one with considerable detachment when he reels off the well-known items—old clothes and family illnesses, holidays and food and friends…Make me stop talking.'

It mattered very little to them where they went, but they walked a lot and saw a few plays. They went to some art galleries. And once they had a picnic.

'It's winter, but the sun never goes in,' he said.

'Except now and then at night. Sydney's like that.'

In the evenings Clea sometimes read aloud to Dan at his suggestion. And he would think: The fire is burning. I am watching her face and listening to her voice. And he felt he knew something eternal that he had always wanted to know. One night Clea read the passage in which Yuri Zhivago, receiving a letter from his wife after their long and tragic separation, falls unconscious.

Because Clea existed and he was in her presence, Dan felt

himself resurrected and so, though what she read was beautiful and he thought so, he laughed with a kind of senseless joy as at something irrelevant when she stopped.

'All right, darling, I suppose it is wonderful. That Russian intensity. If *I* could ever totter to a sofa and collapse with sheer strength of feeling I'd think, Congratulations, Freeman! You're really living.'

Clea laughed, too, but said, 'Ah, don't laugh. Because if you can laugh, you make it impossible...'

One thing Clea could not do was cook. It took Dan some weeks to accept this, because she wasn't indifferent to food. If they ate in a restaurant, she enjoyed a well-chosen meal as much as he did. But when he discovered that she could tackle any sort of diet with much the same enthusiasm he was depressed.

'What do you live on when I'm not around?' he demanded, a little disgruntled.

She thought. 'Coffee.'

He was proud of her. He even liked her a lot. But he couldn't help saying, 'I get hungry.'

She looked abstracted. 'Dan, I—you're *hungry*. Oh...We had steak?'

'Yes, but no—no *trimmings*,' he tried to joke. 'No art.'

'Dan—'

'I take it back about no art.'

'I'll—tomorrow—'

'I take it back about no art.'

'I will do better.'

And after this she tried to cook what she thought were complicated meals for him, and he didn't discourage her.

It was the night they came back from their picnic in the mountains that he had the brilliant idea of asking her why she had never married.

She laughed.

'You wouldn't have had any trouble,' he insisted, trying to see her face.

Still smiling she said, 'The candidates came at the wrong time or they were too young for me when I was young.' She looked at him, raising her brows. 'How old were you? When you married.'

'Twenty-one.'

'I wouldn't have liked you then.'

'You'd have been right. But *you*—tell me.'

She moved restlessly on the sofa, and spread her arms along the back. He felt it was cruel to question her, but he knew he would never stop. She said, 'Oh…I met someone, and bang went five years. Then some time rolled by while I picked myself up. Then I met—someone else who was married. Names don't matter.'

He looked at her.

'All right, they do. But not now…So, by the time you look round after that, you're well into your thirties. And a few of the boys have turned into men, but they're married to girls who preferred them—quite young.'

'Are you saying this to blame me? You are, aren't you?' He heard the rhetorical note in his voice. He knew he had asked her.

Clea seemed to examine the stitches of the black hand-knitted sweater he was wearing. She jumped up quickly and out in the kitchen poured whisky into two glasses, carrying them back.

'I can only say, Clea—if things were different—things would be different...All right, it sounds lame. But I *mean* it. What do you *want* me to do?'

'And what would you *like* me to say? You'll go back to Mary. Do you want me to plead with you?'

He could see that it was neither reasonable nor honourable in him to want that, but in her it would have been more *natural*, he felt. He said so.

Clea was biting the fingernails of her left hand, cagily. He saw again that it was cruel to talk to her like this, but he knew he would never stop.

She glanced at him over her hand. 'You're beginning to think about your old clothes and family holidays, just as I said. And why shouldn't you? These intimate little things are what count in the end, aren't they?'

And she disposed of her hand, wrapping it round her glass as she lifted it from the floor to drink. She rolled a sardonic blue eye at Dan and he gave the impression of having blushed without a change of colour, and frowned and drank, too. Because of course his mind *had* turned lately in that direction. He *had* begun to remember the existence of all that infinitely boring, engulfing domesticity, and his vital but unimportant part in it. It was all *there*, and his. What could he do about it?

Clea knew too much, drank too much, was nervy, pushed herself to excess, bit her fingernails. She was the least conditioned human being he had ever encountered. She was like a mirror held up to his soul. She was intelligent, feeling, and witty. He loved her.

'Many thanks.' But she wouldn't meet his eyes.

'Marriage,' he said, harking back suddenly. 'When I think of it! And you're so independent. What could it give you? Really? No, don't smile.'

Still, she did smile faintly, saying nothing, then said irritatingly, 'Someone to—set mouse traps and dispose of the bodies.'

He brushed this away. 'You hate the office. Why?'

'Dan.' She was patient.

'Why do you hate the office?' He did feel vaguely that he was torturing her. 'Why?'

'I don't see the sun. I lose the daylight hours. The routine's exacting, but the work doesn't matter. It takes all my time from me and I see nothing beautiful.'

'And just what would you do with this time?' he asked,

somehow scientifically. He would prove to her how much better off…

With her left hand, distracted, she seemed to consider the length and texture of the hair that fell over her ear. 'Oh. Look about. Exist.'

Dan thought of Mary. 'Some wives are busy all day long.' He was positive that Mary would be in no way flattered if it were ever suggested that *she* had had time to practise as a student of life. 'In fact,' he went on, 'though cultivation is supposed to be the prerogative of the leisured classes, I think women in your position form a sort of non-wealthy aristocracy all to themselves.'

'Do you?' Clea shifted the dinner plate from her lap and went over to the deal table where she had a lot of paraphernalia brought home from the office spread out. At random she picked up a pencil and tested its point against the cushion of her forefinger, saying, 'That's an observation!'

'No, don't be angry.' He turned eagerly to explain to her over the back of the sofa. 'What I mean is that however busy you are from nine till five, you have all the remaining hours of the day and night to concentrate on yourself—your care, cultivation, understanding, amusement…'

She smiled at him. 'Don't eat that if you can't bear it. I'll make something else.'

He said, 'Forgive me.'

They quarrelled once, one Thursday evening when he

passed on Alan and Joyce Parker's invitation to drive out into the country the following Sunday.

Alan Parker was a tall mild man of fifty, who clerked with dedication among the television films of the library. His wife, whom both Clea and Dan had met at official parties, was friendly and chatty. The Parkers knew Dan was married, and they knew that (as they put it) Dan and Clea had a thing about each other. But they liked Dan because he wasn't disagreeably ambitious, though he was younger than and senior to Alan, and they implied a fondness for Clea. Dan guessed that they would be the subject of Joyce's conversation for a week after the trip, but he couldn't find it in his heart to dislike anyone to whom he could mention Clea's name.

But she said swiftly, 'Oh no, I couldn't go with them.'

He paused, amazed, in the act of kicking a piece of wood back into the fire. 'What do you mean? Why not?'

'No, I just couldn't go,' she said definitely, beginning to look for her place in the book she was holding.

'But *why*?' Dan fixed the fire, buffed some ash from his hands and turned to sit beside her on the sofa. He took the book from her, thrust it behind his back, and forced her to lift her head.

Her look daunted him. He said in parenthesis, 'I'm addicted to that eye shadow.' He said reasonably, 'Only last week you talked about getting out of town.'

'I'd be bored, Dan.'

'Bored? I'd be there!' he rallied her, smiling in a teasing way. 'And Joyce's going to produce a real French picnic lunch.'

There was a smile in her that he sensed and resented.

She said, 'I'm sorry.'

'And *I'm* sorry if the fact that I like to eat one meal a day is offensive to you.'

'Darling. Please go, if you'd like to. No recriminations. Truly.'

Mondays to Fridays he didn't see her all day. He couldn't have borne to lose hours of her company. Six months, he'd had, just days ago. Now there were ten weeks left.

He said unpleasantly, 'You do set yourself up with your nerves and your fine sensibility, Clea. When you begin to feel that a day in the company of nice easygoing people like the Parkers would be unbearably boring, *I* begin to feel you're carrying affectation too far. If you pander to yourself much more you'll find you're unfit to live in that world at all!'

She didn't answer that, or appear to react. Instead she caught his wrist in her right hand and smoothed her thumb against the suede of his watchstrap. 'In their car, Dan, I'd feel imprisoned. I have to be able to get away. I'd be bored, Dan.' She said, 'I don't *love* them!'

He stared, jerked his arm away, gave a short incredulous laugh and stood up. 'Don't *love* them!'

She added, 'As things are.'

Throwing on his coat he went to the door still uttering

sarcastic laughs. 'Don't *love* them! Well—*good*—*night*—*Clea!*'

In ten minutes he returned. And the ten weeks passed.

'Dan? How are you now?' Mary peered down at him, then glanced abruptly right and left, bringing her chin parallel with each of her shoulders in turn. It was dark on the balcony. 'Do you still want your dinner? It'll be ruined, but it's there if you want it…Dan!' She leaned over him.

'What?'

'Well, for heaven's sake, you can still answer when I speak to you! I thought you'd had a stroke or something, sitting there like an image.' She bridled with relief and exasperation.

'No.'

In a brisk admonitory voice she said, 'Well, I think you'd better get yourself along to Dr Webb in the morning. It's all this extra work. And you're not eating. Sometimes I think you don't even know you're home again.'

He said something she couldn't catch.

'What? Where's *what*? Your dinner's in the oven.' Mary waited for him to speak again. 'Smell the garden, Dan…We'd better get ready, then. Jack and Freda'll be over soon.'

'What?' He stirred cautiously in the padded bamboo chair. He felt like someone who has had the top of his head blown off, but is still, astonishingly, alive, and must learn to cope with the light, the light, and all it illuminated.

'I told you this morning,' Mary accused him. 'You hadn't forgotten?'

Carefully he hauled himself up by the balcony railing. 'I'll be bored,' he said.

In the soft black night, Mary went to stand in front of him, tilting her face to look at him. 'Bored, Dan?' She sounded nervous. 'You know Jack and Freda,' she appealed to him, touching his shirtsleeve.

'I don't care for them,' he complained gently, not to her. And added, 'As things are.'

'Oh, Dan!' Mary swallowed. Tears sprang to her eyes. She caught his arm and walked him through the front door, and down the carpeted hall to their bedroom. 'Lie down, Dan. Just lie there.'

He heard her going to the telephone. She rang the doctor. Then she rang Freda and Jack to apologise and ask them not to come. He heard her crying a little with fright as she repeated his uncanny remark in explanation.

And Dan took a deep breath, and looked at the ceiling, and smiled.

10
English Lesson

So after a little indecision, and baring her teeth at the letterbox, Laura posted the letter. It dropped from her fingers, slid out of her control. She felt an instant's black surprise, as if the letter fell in her. Then she thought, Oh well, that's done. And went away from the red letterbox, across the road, and into the park, hearkening all the while to Leslie's difficult conversation. It was about himself. Surrounded by invisible lime trees, skirting the invisible pond and boys playing cricket, he addressed her right ear. She forgot the letter.

It was not important. She did not think it was important. But sensible people thought it was sensible to write it and send it. They sank back with folded hands on hearing that their will had been done, bereft not of the *right* to bully (for what thing is that?) but of the stuff, the wherewithal. Their will was done.

And alack! They were deprived. Their satisfaction was frustration before their very eyes.

As for Laura—touch me not; lay no further words on me. I have gone your way. I am not assailable.

The letter was written, the ground cut from beneath the feet of sensible persons. They champed gloomily and searched as if waiting for specific things, though they were not. Unless the return of their reason for living.

It was only a sort of business letter to a man who was purported to look after Laura's interests. She told him some news and asked for some advice. She had no idea what he was like, but he was purported to be looking after her interests. Anyway, the letter was polite. Laura wondered if it might not be ingenuous. Advisers set their jaws uncertainly when she allowed them to infer this. No, they said tremulously. He has some obligations towards you.

(Had he?)

What else is he for? they insisted.

No one answered.

Laura put discussions and well-phrased paragraphs behind her. After all, this was not the only thing in her life. The doing, the acquiescence, had pacified the country for miles around. Concord—everyone to be, if not happy, at least not looking bitter thoughts at people—is more to some natures than others. She would seem ingenuous, or even quite peculiar if necessary, to any number of businessmen, for concord's sake. It was a question of what mattered most to whom. And how she appeared and what she did mattered little to her. And that obligations were nicely fulfilled in all directions mattered much to others. A bun for a bun.

All that happened was that the man had been given a chance to say: Dear Laura, Yes. (Or, alternatively, No. Or practically anything.) An amiable exchange. Concord. Folded hands. For her—no words. For them—incipient, approaching satisfaction *here*.

And nonexistent.

Propelled by Leslie, the letters skated on the glossy starched tablecloth. Last down for breakfast acting postman, he had delivered mail at five other tables. Laura had watched him: American in a strange land and het up about it. Conspicuous and glad to be. Trying not to seem contemptuous of inferior Anglo-Saxon ways and not succeeding. Bearing his prodigious education heavily. And uneasy. Uneasy.

Airmail striped red, white, and blue. A catalogue with pictures of Italian shoes in it.

Oh. And that one.

Leslie recognised it, too, and languidly expressed his foreknowledge that it contained the most sanguine of replies. He stirred his coffee, and shook salt and pepper over his plate.

Laura read the letter, and her surroundings vanished.

Pausing over his egg, inviting news, Leslie as it were

paused a second time. Yet again he paused and looked at Laura. Then he took the letter up, read it, and replaced it on the table.

Laura's hand lay on her bare collarbone. The bone was scorching. Indeed, her whole body burned, recoiled, retreated from her skeleton. She had been insulted. Someone almost a stranger had hit her across the face. *Why?*

Unable to raise their eyes from the flip little note, the two spoke simultaneously and, it might as well have been, in a language foreign to both and understood by neither. The dining room was submerged fathoms deep. Everything echoed.

What the motive? Where the wit? Why the knife in the ribs? What had she done? Almost total strangers...Surfacing briefly, Laura began to say words in English to Leslie, and he spoke back to her in American, and they were able to hear each other with difficulty, very faintly.

For years unconvincing examples had been reported in books of human beings reeling under blows. Laura reeled, dizzy. Yet she had never been a sheltered person! Still, though she had known real malevolence and survived it, she was awed by the malice of the note. Its very littleness, its unexpectedness, its having less than no reason to it, made it strange.

Her heart hammered. She was insufficiently acquainted with physiology to know what else was happening inside her because of a dozen casual words, but she was learning. For instance, an insult recorded by the eye could cause an entire organism to react as though it had been violently smitten with an axe.

Consider calmly. Had she not been insulted in the old days many times, and borne it with an even mind? Why the fuss now? Today? Yes, but rarely, never by anyone she cared about; never by anyone who cared about her. (She temporarily shelved this remarkable and complicated fact, merely giving it a startled look in passing.) But she and this man did not know each other! No question of emotion one way or the other! Anyway. Anyway, she was grateful to have been reminded what it felt like to be angry. She had forgotten. It was interesting, too, to find that a man could be so…

Oh, was it? Was it? Let the world, the walls of this room, and these rickety bits of furniture understand: she felt herself to have been insulted! What use all this retaliatory chatter with Leslie's American accent over poached eggs? She was anguished, struck back, hacked to the ground. The man's very unknown-ness made it seem that the universe had gratuitously spoken against her.

Nothing but today's lecture would have drawn Leslie from the fascinating case she represented to him. Laura rallied him, urging him to go, groaning soft asides to her spirit till she would be free to attend to its wounds. Reluctantly, he analysed his way to the front door and disappeared. He would like to have been *studied*…

Upstairs, distraught, holding herself with her arms,

stopping now and then to read the note again, Laura trailed about her room.

And yet, wasn't her behaviour extreme? *Think*. A moment's spite, ennui, thought of private troubles, on the part of a man she hardly knew, and this reaction. Come…

Unexpected, uncalled for, unprovoked, unkind, unusual, unbearable…She had a second shower and dressed again. Unusual, unexpected, uncalled for…She looked in no mirrors.

Most peculiar (she addressed herself chattily), but I understand that this is how people start ulcers. Her body was considering whether or not to begin one. A true story she had once heard of a man who had a heart attack and died when his special restaurant table was given to a stranger made sense. If you were old and so indignant, you could die of it.

In the communal kitchen she tried to drown herself with cup after cup of coffee. She ate a large piece of stale cake. In her room, on the bed, she read *The Fall*, splitting her mind neatly in two so that she at one and the same time debated the novel and gently humoured her fevered spirit, whispering softly and soothing it.

She finished that book and started another. Oh, my heart, my heart, she thought, through its pounding. The insult was hours old, yet the heavy thuds would not abate for cake or Camus.

People (the unshaken Laura addressed her languishing body with an increasing hardness and lack of sympathy) are insulted every day. Salesmen. Politicians. All kinds of people. Did they collapse if someone said a brutal word? Did they fall down in the streets? Did they lie about as if their loved one had been seen dropping poison in their porridge? Was this the worst thing that had ever happened to her? Ludicrously far from it! It was trivial. Trivial. Well, then. Enough is enough. The scornful and the wounded both agreed. A moment's grim standing fast.

But unusual, unexpected, unkind, uncalled for, unprovoked, unnecessary…

That man…There had to be some suitable names for him in the language, but her efforts to recall any were strikingly ineffectual. To be natural at all, she saw, she ought to dig up some invective and fling it, at least mentally, at him. She had to *want* to. Leslie had done it for her at breakfast. One of them was wrong—either she or the man. He had a will to be unpleasant; she had no will to name-call. Pig. Lousy thing. *Rude*, she had thought him. He was bloody awful and not nice into the bargain.

Obligations. She had no obligation to pay Mrs Chaloner for the milk. Sandals flapping, unconscious of legs, of mouth with lipstick, she dropped downstairs. A hollow cave. A beating drum.

Money for milk, Mrs Chaloner. I owe you money for milk. She handed it over. Mrs Chaloner stared, but Laura had left her face to its own devices. She was off somewhere under anaesthetic. If her face was grey, if the cheeks cleaved to the bones, if the eyes were glazed and blank, she knew nothing about it.

Upstairs she read the letter again and drank coffee and drifted and was racked with futile wonder. Still her heart pounded. Lying down, she saw it lift the pink blouse she wore, felt its deep unnatural reverberations through her body. Its capacity, for feeling insulted, astonished and exhausted her.

If she were ever to meet him...Are you always so *bad-mannered*? Oh, killing. He would curl up and die. She had a genius for sarcasm. Terrible to unleash a talent like that on a perhaps quite sensitive man!

She moved her head on the pillow restlessly. Death, death...Death, she thought, while her heart struck deafening chimes through her body.

If she were to meet him...

Oh, sickening. Out of all proportion. Too frail for this world. When things *mattered*, she fortunately refrained from this sort of performance. It was ridiculous beyond words in the person who had lived her life. Face it. To mind *this* much you have to be megalomaniac. No. Just—just...It was not *right*. Think what he said! Oh, what he said, what he said. The burning smoking strokes of her heart continued. The very bed shook under them.

Laura! Laura!

Disembodied, she jerked herself up and meandered to the landing. Yes?

A drink for you, gasped Mrs Chaloner, looking at her amazed. I thought you might be able to do with it. It's so hot. Here.

She offered up a clinking tumbler, icy, lemony, ginny. She was kind.

Oh, thank you! How kind of you! If ever I need anything! Laura said with alarming vivacity.

It's so hot up here, Mrs Chaloner told her.

Laura gazed about in a vague stupor. Yes, it is, she agreed insincerely, beginning at once to sweat now that the fact was pointed out.

Indeed it was hot. It was roasting, boiling, and had been for hours. Laura simmered slowly, drinking the icy drink, burning, hammering, and insulted.

Sagging, far from convalescent, she sat on the edge of her bed. Through the window she could see children playing on the lawn of a distant school. Little did they know…Shock. That was all that was wrong. Brandy, blankets, a St Bernard dog…No, sweet tea, blankets…But could shock have the effect of bringing about a permanent physical change? Could she doubt it? Everything about her, physical and metaphysical, had sunk, shrunk. She was shorter, pruned, slightly murdered.

The world, human beings. Her mind reviewed every fact she had ever learned. She recollected all the significant scenes of her life, and the meaningful words. She contemplated the perfect love that casts out fear, rested in it, knowing that to be reality and herself to be, in truth, beyond harm. Smiled.

But just the same...

Dinnertime, and Leslie returned to his room along the corridor and to the table. All day, in his mind, he had written letters to that guy. He stated doubtfully his opinion that Laura would survive. Then he repeated it. Appointing himself chief distracter and analyst, he distracted and analysed while the undiverted heart thumped.

Late that night, when she was alone, the banging stopped quite suddenly. Hurt pride and vanity, her whole vast sense of the dreadful wrongness of what had happened, up in smoke. The heart that knew how to act temperately in crucial situations gave up being a burning mountain on this inappropriate occasion, and was all at once lightless.

I know something, Laura thought before falling dead asleep. It did not speak against me; it spoke to me. And I know what insulted means. I was never insulted before. I'll never be insulted again. I'll always know what insulted means. As I know what some other words mean.

11

It Is Margaret

Before the ceremony began, the woman with hairy legs and an air of having just abandoned a cigarette wandered as though at a party to the coffin where—though it was impossible and not so—Clelia's mother, Margaret, was. Three days ago, four days ago, Clelia had said to her mother, 'Come and see the blossom I've brought back.' She had just returned to Sydney after a three-week absence in the mountains.

'Can't it come to me?'

'No,' she said gaily, insistently, not thinking really, never wondering. 'No, you'll have to come out here. It's so tall. I can't move the vase.'

So her mother left her chair in Clelia's sitting room and walked through to the kitchen, where the bower of japonica and peach and pear blossom was.

After the two-hour weekly visit permitted by Theo they said goodbye beside the car in the black soft night.

'I'll hear from you before you go away next week?' her mother asked, knowing, saying nothing.

'Of *course*. Naturally.'

'I do feel old tonight,' her mother said, knowing.

'No.' She smiled and hugged her. 'No, you're not.'

Uneasy, affronted, the minister approached her and leaned down, referring to the woman with the hairy legs now swaying past the coffin, reading the cards on the sweet spring flowers. 'Who is that?'

'No one,' Clelia said. In truth she was a stranger, heard of, but met now for the first time, wife of one of Theo's associates.

Over. Outside on swept gravel. Over, over. A young man spoke to her and wiped his eyes. Others spoke. Clelia and Stephanie, her mother's cousin, walked towards the car. Another friend said, 'I must get home to my family.' Some you might have counted on were afraid of catching death.

'Of course.'

So Clelia drove with Stephanie to the house where her mother had lived, almost from the time she was girl. She had remained a girl for a long time, which is only to say that she kept a sort of innocence and trust, and resisted knowing what she knew. It was the measure of her strength, so gentle-seeming, that, when she did face what she knew, her nature was unchanged. That is, she lacked all inclination to wound and was not bitter. She had made a grievous mistake, beyond repairing. She accepted this, but failed to become a worse person. That had been Theo's aim, to reduce her as a human being, to make her over in his image.

Clelia thought of her stepfather, Theo. He was a great figure in his own imagination. Theo…'From the Greek,' he used to say, and laugh. Clelia had not seen him for ten years till today, had never been back to the house. It had been safest for her mother, who had become, anyway, too ill, too worn, to leave him, that he should never see mother and daughter together. He was jealous. Her mother could have no friends, no relations, no pets, nothing but Theo. He got easily jealous if he was not ever and ever attended to first and only. So he always was.

And perhaps there was some justification for his jealousy. Clelia had never known how to describe him to any new acquaintance, lover, asking about her life. What was there to say? She could only move her body, turn her head, breathe in, aware of seeming evasive. There was too much; it was too stark: it would take too long. No one wanted sad stories. Theo had been a tyrant, terrifying in her childhood and girlhood, a man who tortured and smiled and, after her escape, continued in this role in her mother's life. It sounded excessive, unbelievable, so she said nothing.

She had no idea what he could have seemed to himself, but he could be seen to act and calculate. He had noticed his exceptional power to cause unhappiness and fear. He had also noticed, certainly, his power over Clelia's mother, and drawn conclusions flattering to his vanity. Those simple others out there in the world, occasionally encountered even in his domain, smiled and performed tiny deeds inspired by compassion or affection, their eyes watchfully on him. But he, Theo, going his own way, *got his own way*. Others tried to please, but he won.

Before the service she had met him face to face, the leading actor once of all her nightmares. His face was crumpled. He cried. Long ago Clelia had streamed with tears for her mother's life; there had been streams and years of tears. But now it felt true—what poets said: hearts turned to stone. There was no further harm Theo could do. He had done his worst. The crimes had been committed.

Two neighbours had driven him back to her mother's house after the funeral. They were there with him when Clelia arrived. Thoughtfully, one of the neighbours had baked cakes and biscuits, and made tea and set it out. They all held cups and looked into them.

Theo sat blowing his nose. 'I can't believe it,' he said, choking.

Even to Clelia it seemed possible that everything could yet be reversed. Since it was all so sudden and recent, with every least incident so clear, with cause and effect so clear, the hideous wrongness with which everything had happened seemed to shout in the room, demanding instant action, instant reversals.

'Now, Theo…' The neighbours watched him because he was dangerous. 'We've put some dinner in the oven for you.'

'I'll come back tomorrow,' Clelia said. 'We'll talk about things then. The doctor will call in this evening to see you.' She rose and one of the neighbours, a widow, went with them to the door.

'He's a cruel man,' she told Clelia, sparing her nothing. 'He made your mother cry. Even when she was ill, he'd go on and on, driving her to do everything exactly as he ordered. The cruellest man I ever knew.'

Clelia listened with no expression. Who could tell her about Theo?

In her flat the telephone rang and rang. When somebody dies suddenly the lives of survivors explode; hours are minutely cluttered. The telephone rang.

'Oh, Sam. My mother's died. Suddenly. No, I can't see you. No, don't come over. The telephone keeps ringing. No, I don't want any dinner. No, I'm not alone. Steph's staying for a while. She's brought some work.'

She told Stephanie, 'Sam's coming over. He wants me to go to dinner.'

In most intricate detail, in case he should know the magic

that would reverse all, she told Sam with passionate fluency of the accidents, delays, absences, mismanagement, leading to her mother's death.

Sam understood it all, looking at her carefully. He told her, 'I'm taking you out for a meal.'

'I'm not hungry.'

'Eat anyway.'

The suburban shopping centre that she had passed a thousand times—milk bar, delicatessen, wine bar. All there exactly as they had been on Friday when she brought the blossom down from the mountains, and insisted...

'What's going to happen to *him*?' Sam wanted to get it clear.

'He has a family in England, from another marriage. He visited them. He didn't ruin *their* lives. Their mother left him when they were almost babies. It's their turn now. But it's too late. He can't do anything else to my mother now. He actually asked if I would like to go and live with him and look after him. I could have anything, if I would.'

'You're not going?' He looked incredulous.

'Oh, *Sam*...But till arrangements are made, I'll go down and make his dinner and fix the laundry. Steph will come with me. I couldn't go alone.'

Sam stopped and grabbed her arm. In the window of a gift shop a frilly red lamp was meaninglessly shining. 'You're not going to do his washing?'

'I was going to put it into the machine.' She was vague.

'No, you're not. Send it to a laundry.' Sam was outraged somehow. 'Now I'm serious. Promise you will.'

'Oh…All right.' She was unused to being told what to do, but if it mattered to anyone about Theo's washing she would certainly send it to the laundry.

At the small unlicensed French restaurant up the street, where retired couples, isolated persons, regularly ate, Clelia sat with Sam. He told her what she should eat and ordered it. He then settled down to the history of the Russian Revolution. Clelia had so much to think about. She knew so little about the revolution, and he knew so much. Why now did he feel it vital to pass all this news on to her? Most of her life she'd thought, since no one else was like Theo, everyone was delicate, full of sensibility. Now she knew this to be wildly untrue. But some people really were, and Sam—so large, so towering—was towards her, indeed, exceedingly considerate. Therefore, although it was like having a steel rake dragged through her mind, with her whole nature turned to the undoing of mistakes, the return to Friday and restoration of her mother to life, she responded distractedly to Sam's talk of revolution, great waves of history battering her head, centuries rushing past.

Late every day she and Stephanie went down the steps to her mother's house. Everything was unreal—cement steps, sky, absent presence, new ingratiating Theo. Perhaps he, too, thought her mother might return. He was deeply unwilling to leave the country and go to his vaunted sons and daughters, but agreed when he had no choice, he who had granted no choices.

That first evening of the dinner ritual he greeted them with extraordinary smiles and then, looking about in case they might be overheard, so that Stephanie and Clelia, too, glanced over their shoulders, he led them inside. 'This way, this way.'

Darting ahead, then rushing back, he led them through the sunroom, through his small study, through the kitchen, through the square hall, into her mother's bedroom. There he stood, bright-eyed, expectant, full of secrets.

Still the women stood. 'Wait, wait!' He rushed about the room, lowering blinds, drawing curtains. 'Now, come, come.' With commanding gestures he indicated that he wanted help to move the bed. Glancing blankly over at Stephanie (because what that he did could surprise them now?), she helped him edge it out from the wall.

'Good, good! Now, wait.' Looking furtively about, Theo dropped to his knees, felt under the edge of the carpet and came up with his hand full of diamonds—rings, earrings, brooches. 'There! She left them to you, didn't she? Look after them. Hide them away.'

Bemused, Clelia took them from him. Diamonds. Diamonds. Blossom alive in the kitchen a mile away, diamonds winking under the carpet and now in the palm of her hand.

Stones. The person because of whom they all stood there, gone. *It is Margaret you mourn for...*

It was very odd. They sat about and talked to Theo while he ate the dinner they had cooked, and there was never a violent or malicious word. There was no hostage any more. He could not hold Clelia or her mother hostage any more, and he understood that. No one had to pander to him any more. But if he was capable of understanding so much now, it was horribly confirmed that he had known *then* what he was doing.

He asserted, 'We never had any troubles like other couples. Nothing ever went wrong with us.'

Sometimes, in the first week of that month before he left the country forever, he did eye Clelia and appear inclined to haggle about the furniture.

'I'm not sure,' he would say, watching her cagily. 'I think *I* bought the sofa, and the television set.' Then, carried away, he would list every item in sight.

'All right. None of it was hers.'

'That's right,' he would say, disingenuously, triumphant, the Theo of old.

Less than a week, and all those tears, and all those lies about their halcyon life, and all this cunning thought expended on the furniture! On bits of wood whose only intrinsic value lay in their having been tended for years by such a person as Clelia's mother. In detective stories wooden people argued over wills and tables and chairs. Clelia had never imagined it happened in real life—that after a death survivors schemed to grab possessions—but it would all happen now, if she cared to play these games of Theo's choosing.

'It's all yours, then.'

'That's right.' Perplexed by his easy triumph, he smiled at her.

'Maybe,' he conceded, giving Clelia a canny look, 'maybe she owned that one chair.' He cleared his throat and studied her.

'Oh, the chair. Okay.' She paused. 'Will you have some ice-cream now?'

He could see that she wasn't going to play, and it made him feel discontented when he wanted to jump on them and crow, order them about, and they wouldn't play. It wasn't fair. He was clever. He was master. Almost always he had been able to manoeuvre them in the old days. Clelia and her mother. It was his only fun. Otherwise he got so bored. They had been so funny in the old days. So natural. Looking with such big startled eyes. He stupefied them so. They almost fell over backwards. They almost cringed away from him. It was so funny. They couldn't make him out at all. However they reacted, it had made him want to laugh secretly. He knew how they hated it. With his eyes gleaming, he had sucked in their reactions. He knew that his gleaming look, his smile no less than his words, deliberate pauses, were a sort of torment. Meat and drink, meat and drink. But those days were all over long ago. Clelia had gone long ago. Now they had both left him.

Now there was only Clelia pretending not to care that he was winning the furniture from her. She *must* care, but she wouldn't give him the satisfaction, and he *wanted* the satisfaction. He wanted the reassurance. His whole life had gone into getting: getting goods, getting ascendancy. If at this late time everyone refused to submit, refused to acclaim his rightness in all things, it was very dangerous for him. Somewhere he might have made a serious miscalculation, and that could not be. It was his right to dominate and win.

In the mornings there were countless telephone calls, cables to be sent, doctors to talk to, accounts to be paid, solicitors, agents, banks. Stephanie and Clelia drove Theo to and fro when he had business that had to be attended to in person. He did get agitated sometimes, but he *was* old. In the evenings they returned to make dinner.

After the first days had passed Theo began to change. Clelia would go at night to the house and unpack her basket of shopping and find that, in the course of the day, Theo had been thinking. He would say, 'I've been thinking,' and pause tremendously. 'I think that table belonged to your mother,' or, 'I think that silver tray was hers.'

Every day an object that was in truth her mother's was offered up, turned over to Clelia. What those relinquished objects represented in terms of change, probably only Stephanie, her mother's cousin, of all her friends, understood.

Stephanie had seen Theo if not in his heyday, in the final period, anyway, of his prime.

'I never used to believe what you said about him. I thought you were inflating him into a monster to make yourself interesting.'

But it was no exaggeration, as Stephanie now knew. He had tormented out of existence someone generous and loving, and had amazed anyone in his power; there was no predicting his moods—sometimes joking, more often glaring, black, bullying.

That he might lose anything of value in his stampede, profoundly indifferent as he was to the means used to conquer, never seemed to occur to him. He was never happy. But at least he was dangerous to other people and their chances of happiness. That was something. Clelia broke away at last, perceiving that Theo was not a fate imposed by the gods, perceiving that there was no sense or virtue in co-operating with a nature that clearly saw nothing good, and intended nothing good. He had done his worst.

When Theo ate his dinner and she and Stephanie talked to him, drinking tea, drinking coffee to keep him company, she drank with one of her life's teachers. He was a force of nature. She couldn't have imagined him if she hadn't known him. She would have known much less about good and evil without his lessons, but she had paid a great deal for them. Having learned, she could have moved on, but because her mother was held as surety his presence had remained, though unseen, pervasive in her life as a serious illness.

So they passed the sugar bowl and stirred.

Often, while she grew daily thinner with unfelt strain, Clelia had to laugh. Theo made her laugh, and Stephanie laugh, as he ate his dinner. He laughed so much that he had to gasp and wipe his eyes. They laughed themselves speechless and weak. None of them could remember afterwards what started them off. Sometimes Theo laughed so much that he was quite unable to convey what was in his mind. Catching laughter from him, the others would say, laughing, 'What? What *is* it?'

'Oh, I can't—' he would gasp, waving his arms at them, and rolling about in his chair.

Exhausted and dazed, they would emerge from these overpowering bursts of mirth and part at the door, Clelia and Stephanie taking away baskets, letters to post, notebooks full of lists for the following day.

With a new, childish good nature, Theo would stand at the door, waving and calling messages.

But Clelia had been a child more recently than Theo, and at first an excessively trusting one; she and her mother had fallen again and again into traps disingenuously prepared. Theo had many tricks and faces.

'What is it, do you think?' Stephanie would ask, on the way home. Theo had never been famous as a laugher. This seemed very peculiar.

'Do you think it's a symptom?' Clelia asked, wrinkling her forehead anxiously. 'Is it some sort of mania?'

But since Clelia had been ten or eleven, most things Theo had said and done had undoubtedly been symptoms of nothing good, so that now it was difficult to judge. 'When someone is so different from everyone else, you can't tell what's happening.'

Their powers of reasoning had somehow to be suspended in Theo's presence. They felt stupefied. He had often, in the past, been gratified to notice this effect he had on people.

In Clelia's kitchen the blossom began to fall. In her mother's house she had to open drawers, wardrobes. Everywhere, in the most remote cupboard, each object was fresh, carefully placed. Jovial, bluff, the doctor said to Clelia on the telephone, 'We'll get him on a plane. Don't worry. If I have to push him in a wheelbarrow.' On an entirely different note, he added sadly before hanging up, 'The wrong one died.'

Each day now, as the day of the flight sped towards them, Theo wanted to take less and less. From making off with every last teaspoon, he now could scarcely bother to take his own clothes.

'At least take your radio. At least take your binoculars,' Clelia said.

'Oh, I don't know. Don't you want them?'

'Not really, Theo.'

He had no heart for anything. Clelia was the last sign. *She* was what he wanted, but she was no longer a possession to be packed.

Stephanie drove Clelia to the house on the last day. Theo was waiting, packed, with clothes, with money, with deeds to property, and yet like a refugee with nothing.

'Quick! Quick! I want to show you something. Come in here.' Secretive, he led them through to the sitting room. 'Now, wait there.'

Outside the mynas called noisily. Up at the junction on the main road to the city traffic was ceaseless.

'What now?' Stephanie widened her eyes.

Clelia shook her head, and Theo returned with a big envelope and sat down on the sofa next to her. With shaking hands, he fumbled in the envelope, then carefully drew out a photograph, a studio portrait of a young man. 'I was twenty when that was taken. Not bad, eh? Would you like it?' He seemed wistful. He watched her face.

Clelia hesitated. 'Oh, Theo...You should take it with you. For your family.'

Restlessly he moved about. '*They* won't want it. I want *you* to have it.'

Here it was again—the mystery that pursued her through life in one form, in another, returning and returning, presenting itself relentlessly for her solution: how should human beings treat each other? How to treat Theo now? How to treat people who, when the opportunity was theirs, ill-treated you?

How not to be overcome again and again by an aggressor if you were unwilling to meet blow with blow?

Neither her own considerable experience, nor the theories of others, the thinkers of centuries, solved it easily, once and for all, or even in a particular instance. Theo and his varied kind jumped instinctively on anyone down. They gained power from the 'understanding' and 'compassion' of others, counted on some such weak-mindedness, soft-heartedness, without understanding remotely the movements of thought and feeling from which they sprang. Benefit showered down, regardless of understanding, as if generous or magnanimous natures were part of the public utilities. Arguing in this way with herself, Clelia often concluded that such natures even *might* be part of the public utilities, magnanimity provided as tap water, electricity are provided. The alternative to *seeming* to cave in, to *seeming* overborne, was to deny oneself, become one with the aggressor, offer the final tribute. Theo destroyed the person closest to him, her mother. The worse overcame the better; the worse, the greater.

Theo sat with his own image in his hand, to some extent in her power. But what puny gesture of hers could do more than trivialise the past? A pettish or spiteful jab to Theo's ego would in its pointlessness insult the true tragedy a feeble gesture of rejection would be meant to avenge, even to point out to the forgetful Theo, with his memories of 'no troubles'.

This mystery was so familiar to Clelia, had so often before

demanded her attention, as though it were her most particular task in life to understand this fully, that her myriad reflections took place simultaneously in the time of receiving from Theo's hand his studio portrait, and then five or six others.

She held them.

He said, 'I want you to have them. Would you like them?' And, reaching across, he shuffled through them.

Clelia said yes to every one.

Theo seemed very pleased, proud, and almost grateful. 'There, then!'

He looked at her and, since she had already done more than she could do, Clelia met his eyes.

12

A Few Days in the Country

'Heavens!' Sophie put her suitcase down on the concrete path and watched the cat flatten itself under a daphne bush and disappear.

'I don't know why she does that,' Caroline said, looking after it abstractedly.

'I don't usually terrify cats.'

'No, it isn't you.' Caroline led the way up the broad steps to her house. 'She always acts as if she thinks someone's going to murder her.'

Knocking Sophie's bag against the wall as she went ahead in a nervous rush, Caroline stopped at the entrance to a bedroom with two big windows and a view of eucalypt-covered hillside. She looked anxiously about. 'Is this all right?

Perhaps I should have given you the other room?'

'Caroline, *no*. This is lovely. It was so kind of you to let me come.' And Sophie, who thought she never blushed, blushed from waist to forehead, and turned to give the oblongs of countryside her polite attention.

'I *asked* you.'

Drawing a dubious breath, Sophie saw imposed on the wooded slope another landscape of such complexity that she could think of no one thing to say.

Caroline straightened the Indian rug, then eyed her guest, and went on laboriously, 'How are you, anyway? Now that we're established.'

'Oh, extremely healthy, as always.' Sophie heard the sudden liveliness in her own voice, felt herself brim, for Caroline's benefit, with something resembling animation and high spirits. Apart from the fact that none of this was true, she could see it must seem a little odd that someone as fine as all that should have taken up in so urgent a fashion—involving trunk calls and telegrams—an invitation given warmly, but on the spur of the moment, months before in Sydney. They had friends in common. Caroline was a widow, a doctor, and lived alone in this small country town. She was grey-haired, sturdy and, Sophie felt, mildly fantastic. Sophie herself was a pianist. This was almost all they knew about each other.

By way of explanation, Sophie now repeated, as she blindly snapped open the locks of her case, what she had said in yesterday's calls. 'Suddenly the city just—got me down. A few free days turned up and I thought, if you don't mind…'

This was so far from being a characteristic impulse that she hardly knew how to account for herself. The universe was hostile. The sun rose in the west. She was in danger. Only strangers might not be malevolent. Something like all this was wrong.

'Mind!' Caroline clapped her hands to her head, then fixed her springy hair behind her ears. 'If you knew how we like to be visited! Now, come and have lunch. Then we'll produce some of this famous country air for you. Scoot around in the car. There were mushrooms out the other day.'

'Really?'

They both smiled and relaxed slightly.

Sophie was not surprised to find that the mushrooms had been claimed by hungrier souls since Caroline first noticed them, but there was a wonderful cloud-streaked sky, a river, and waves of little hills to the horizon. Completing Caroline's circular tour, they returned to the house, took rugs on to the grass, and lay in the shade of a pear tree drinking iced coffee and losing control of the Sunday papers.

'You won't see much of me. I'm missing all day and sometimes half the night, so you'll have the place to yourself. Mrs Barratt comes in to tidy up. Oh, and I forgot to show you the piano. Mr Crump tuned it yesterday as a special favour.

Came out of retirement!'

'Caroline.' Sophie looked at her in dismay. 'All this trouble you've gone to. So kind. It makes me feel—'

'What?'

'Terrible. False colours, false pretences.'

'I'll expect to hear of hours of practice when I get back every night,' Caroline continued firmly.

'But I wasn't going to practise. I don't practise much any more. I'm—getting lazy,' she improvised.

Caroline glanced at her quickly, then thumped at a party of scavenging ants with a folded newspaper. 'Of course you'll practise.'

Sophie shook her head. 'Truly. It doesn't matter. Music's not the most important thing in the world.' She gazed down the grassy slope and up to the hills in the distance.

'The most important thing in the world!' Scornful, roused, Caroline asked, 'What is?'

'Ah, well...' Sophie's voice had no expression. She did know.

But such a statement struck Caroline as merely silly. Quite apart from medicine, the world was full of causes, calls to effort. The list in her mind was endless. Even the imminent perfecting of man through education was not a thing she had doubts about.

The women eyed each other with goodwill and an aware-ness that they were natural strangers. The views of persons like that could not be taken seriously. It was almost a relief. They talked about politics and local controversies, and it scarcely mattered at all what anyone said.

'You see!' Caroline stopped herself in mid-flight. 'There's no one here to argue with except a few old cronies. So I rush back to Sydney every month, go round the galleries, and see some plays. Try to keep up…'

Sophie realised that she was at least partly in earnest, and felt a pang of appalled compassion as she habitually did now at what interested people, at the trouble they took to act in the world, move. If only they knew!

'I'm going to leave you in peace now while I do some weeding. It's the Sunday ritual.' Caroline stood up, looking resolutely about the big garden.

How courageous! What fortitude! Pity moved in Sophie and she got to her knees, ready to stand. 'Let me help. I can weed, or anything.' There was so much Caroline and everyone must never know.

'Stay there. You're on holiday. You can do some watering later.' Preoccupied already, Caroline disappeared round the corner of the house, and Sophie sank back horizontal on the rug, and the light went out of her. Tears came to her eyes and she wiped them away and sat up again.

Her instruction resumed at full volume. Phrases that were by now only symbols indicating the devastation caused by grief transfixed her attention. The instruction had been going on for several months now. When she was in company or asleep, the volume was reduced, but the question and answer, the statements below the level of thought, never really stopped. A massive shock. A surprise of great magnitude. 'A great surprise,' she repeated obediently.

In its way, the instruction was trying to save her, Sophie supposed. It wanted her to live. She humoured this innocent desire, attending to its words as though it were a kind, stupid teacher.

To be or not to be. Her lips half-smiled. Out in the world, when she lived out in the world, she had been stringently trained: nothing about herself, her life, her death, was worth taking seriously. Sophie smiled again. No wonder humankind could not bear much reality. The things that happened.

Caroline crossed the lawn, purposeful and silent, grasping secateurs. A long interval followed, during which only bees and shadows and leaves moved in the garden. The green tranquillity wavered and shifted in the currents of air. Sophie's heart jumped about in disorder as it often did now as the cat suddenly fled past her, out of a shady ambush. Patches of her forehead and head froze with fright. She took a deep breath and tried to stifle the bumping in her chest. Only the cat. Only Caroline's poor cat.

'Puss? Puss?' Her tone compelled the cat to acknowledge

her presence. 'Don't be frightened. How nervous you are. Everything's all right.'

The stricken animal thawed and fled, leaving only a haunted path. Sophie mourned for it, mourned for its view of her as an object potentially powerful and evil, hardened. How wise are you, cat, to resist my blandishments, my tender voice, my endless—I would have you think—capacity for kindness. It *is* almost endless, too. I would never hurt you, except by accident, and hardly even then. But, oh, how sad I am, cat.

Her mouth smiled at 'sad'.

'You look very contented and peaceful there,' Caroline said, wandering over to her. 'That's good. Means you're settling in. Who volunteered to water the garden while I make some dinner?'

Syringa, woodbine, japonica, tangled cascades of roses hanging from old fences. Sophie wandered, trailing the hose, its silver spray hissing gently. Daylight was fading from moment to moment, the air cooling. Magpies held a dialogue as they flew, swooping low. Hearing them, Sophie told herself: I'm in the bush.

Then suicide thought of her. Unlike the instruction, which was of a labyrinthine complexity, suicide used simple words and images and, when it overcame the instruction and claimed her in a tug of war, it used them ceaselessly. Suicide was easy provided the balance of your mind was not disturbed. The essential point, neglected by faint hearts, was to commit the deed in a place where you would not soon be discovered. You would leave the city, taking with you a quantity of pain-killing drugs or sleeping pills. You would post one or two letters before catching the train, because it would be cruel never to let yourself be found. And there were the reasons, the reasons you were dying for...Which no one wanted to know and would prefer never to understand, anyway...Then you would board a train going in a direction previously chosen, climb out at the selected station, walk to a secluded spot, lie down, and swallow the tablets. Having taken care, of course, to bring water.

Sophie sighed. A crude, peculiar, *material* way of dealing with extreme unhappiness. Like wars. Beside the point.

'What will you have to drink? Whisky? There's everything.' Caroline stood at the front door looking out remotely at the sky and the darkening garden.

'Thank you. Yes. I was watching the light on the hills there.'

'Lovely. You've brought good weather. Whisky, then. Don't stay out in the cold.'

'I'll just put the hose away.'

Light came on in the house. As Sophie went along the side path, she felt the consoling silence all about. Silence lay enormous behind the sound of her footsteps on grass, the dragging hose, late bird cries, insect scrapings.

Because, the argument resumed, being dead was not what

she wanted most. It was the only alternative. Just as, presumably, generals did not want, first and foremost, dead bodies and buildings fallen down.

Over dinner Caroline, who had emerged as funny, generous, and Christian, asked about their Sydney friends and showed an inclination to dissect them as though they were interesting cadavers. Dismay ground Sophie to an almost total stop when this disloyalty displayed itself. Any betrayal, of whatever order, instantly related itself to the great calamities of the world. Which of these had not originated in one person? Her knife and fork grew heavy in her fingers, and it was an effort to breathe. Her dear friends! Unfitted to judge though she might be—no Christian—she knew she would judge Caroline later. Though even dear friends were now like faded frescoes. That response in their defence was only an outdated reflex. It was of no consequence that they would never meet again, so how should Caroline's mild malice disturb?

While Sophie drooped over her dinner, Caroline grew more and more inclined to ramble, and finally rambled right out of the field of friendship into small-town scandal—unfrocked ministers and cows that ate free-growing marijuana.

'Everyone drinks their milk. Can you wonder at the things that go on here?'

Sophie laughed with relief, a little too long.

✳

In the morning Caroline left for the hospital at seven. Sophie showered, dressed, and brushed her hair, advancing jerkily from one operation to the next. No one and nothing could be relied on now. Nothing was automatic. The simplest habits had deserted. Everything took thought, yet thought was what she had nothing to spare of. Because she had so much to think about and it was so important. And nobody realised.

Wandering through to the kitchen, she made some toast and coffee and set it out on the back veranda in the sun. The grey cat appeared at the door and saw her, coffee cup raised to lips, and after a moment's paralysis slunk off like a hunted thing. Sophie called after it in a beseeching voice, then rose and went to stand in the doorway. She spoke to the breathing garden, hoping the cat could hear, but there was no sign of it. When the dishes were washed, she trundled out the lawnmower and mowed some square yards of Caroline's dewy grass. The day was beautiful.

It was rather feeble to attempt suicide and fail. It definitely placed a person's good faith in doubt. It was worse to make an attempt with the conscious intention of not succeeding. Anyway. Anyway, she felt contempt for suicide. Butcher yourself? Why should you? Fall into a decline because nothing was what it seemed? Some had ambitions perhaps to enter the higher reaches of blackmail. But Sophie had never thought of suicide. It was just that lately she could not stop thinking about it.

Little ridges of grass that had escaped her stood conspicuous. She pushed the mower to and fro, stopping once to throw off her sweater. Only a psychosis could make the deed anything but (Sophie pushed the mower so hard that it was airborne) pusillanimous. Pusillanimous. And had she any desire to be that?

Worn out by the violence of her repudiation, she stopped for an indignant breath. Then nervously ran the four fingers of her left hand across her forehead. It was just a fact that she wasn't safe, wasn't safe yet. And all you had to do was not be found too soon…

Small black ants were swarming over her bare feet and ankles. She stamped about, brushing the tenacious ones away, dropping the handle of the mower. Bent right over, hair hanging, her glance slanted suddenly sideways: the cat sat under a bush some yards away, watching with round yellow eyes.

Cautiously, Sophie lowered herself to the ground, sat motionless on the grass, exchanging eyes with the cat. Then she began very gently to talk to it, and the cat listened, for the first time showing no fear.

Sophie looked vaguely into its green retreat, and rested her cheek on her knee. She closed her eyes. It was the tone of voice, she told herself. Cats must be susceptible to voices. And there was a slight, but temporary, amelioration of her suffering.

It was not a thing you could do, not in an immediate, noticeable way. It was not considerate to wreck other people's lives for no better reason than that you would prefer to be dead. Wreck? Well, perhaps that did overstate the case. Inconvenience, she amended.

'What a pity!' Sophie muttered. 'What a pity!' It was hard to understand, something she could never be reconciled to. Real love was not so common even in so large a place as the world.

Mortal wounds, the instruction said. The psychic knife went in; the psychic blood came out...

My own doing, Sophie reflected, while the instruction rattled on in the background monotonously. It was she who had done the empowering, delivered herself over. Nothing she had previously understood or learned had prepared her. Yet her life had never been sheltered. Again now, the magnitude of her surprise, of her mistake, bore down on her. Public violence, bombs, wars were this private passion to destroy made manifest on a large scale.

'That grass is wet, Sophie. I have to call on old Mr Crisp out past the church, so I came in to see if you were all right.'

As Caroline emerged from the tunnel of honeysuckle and may, Sophie scrambled up uncertainly, rubbing damp hands and cut grass on her damp slacks. 'Oh, Caroline...I was mowing the grass...I was talking to the cat.'

'Did she let you?'

'In a way. Almost.'

'I don't think there's time, or we could have a cup of tea together. Walk back up to the car with me, anyway. I only looked in. She was operated on once, poor Cat, and I'm convinced the vet was led astray by curiosity. He'd just qualified. She lost faith in the human race.'

Leaf mould lay thick beneath the trees.

'How awful,' Sophie said.

'Mmm.' Caroline frowned at the path for a few steps, then looked up briskly, glancing at her watch. 'You could try feeding her if you want to be friends. There's plenty of stuff in the fridge.'

'I don't think she's hungry.'

Her right hand on the gate, Caroline paused. Sophie looked at this small tough hand and waited obediently. She had the impression that she was expecting a message, and that perhaps Caroline was the person who was going to deliver it to her.

But Caroline just said absently, 'No, it isn't that. It's a bit demoralising to have her flitting about like the victim of a vivisectionist. Which she is. I really wondered if I'd find you practising. I was going to creep off. It isn't right, Sophie, that you should throw away your talents.'

Though once upon a time she herself had said this sort of thing to encourage other people, Sophie smiled with a sort of heartless gaiety. 'Did you really come back for that?'

'I did indeed. You practise, my girl, or we'll turn you into a medico and send you overseas to do good.' Her concern, which seemed real enough, disinterested, made Sophie feel ashamed of her own duplicity, though the concern was so misplaced and even preposterous that she laughed aloud.

'How can you think it matters, Caroline? Talent. Playing pianos. And even give it priority over doing good?' She felt tremendously amused, full of laughter.

'Just get on with it!' With a minatory nod, Caroline made for her little yellow car, and Sophie waited and waved through the familiar grating and humming of gears; then Caroline was gone, and so was the hilarity that had felt so permanent.

Alone again, Sophie conversed with herself about the weather as though to distract an invalid acquaintance. But, really, the light *was* dazzling, like the first morning of the world. Radiance pealed across Caroline's small valley from sky to dandelion. After staring into it for a time, Sophie continued back along the path to the uneven square of cut grass. Safely there, and gazing as if to count the blades, it seemed to her that something as mesmeric, as impersonal, and of the same dimensions as the sun was before her eyes. And this was the instruction.

'The Coopers and Stephen rang to say how much they enjoyed the other night.' Caroline looked up from the telephone directory.

'How punctilious! They were nice.' On her way to the

kitchen with a large copper vase, Sophie paused.

'You were a great success.'

'I liked them, too.'

Caroline began to turn the pages distractedly. 'I'm looking for that new garage man who took Alec's place. The car's due for an oil change.' She sighed and let the book fall shut. 'I'll call in when I'm passing. It's a shame you have to go tomorrow. There's no reason to rush away.'

'I do work,' Sophie reminded her. 'Someone's going to notice I'm not there.' While she would almost certainly be nowhere, there was no reason to burden Caroline with that information.

'I daresay.'

'You've been marvellous.'

With Caroline gone, chains dropping from her, Sophie sank from the platform in space where it was laid on her to make conversation and act as if she believed in the great conspiracy. It was amazing what quantities of time could be passed out there when necessary, she reflected, filling the vase with fresh water. Some people spent the whole of their lives there without even knowing it. Like Ivan Ilyich and innumerable other characters who crowded to suggest themselves. Sophie clasped her hands round the cold vase and rushed through to the sitting room, leaning slightly backwards to avoid the spreading branches of japonica. Placing the vase carefully on the low table by the windows she escaped from the house to the open air, and stood bathed in surprise.

Here was the real world you could never remember inside houses: soft rounded hills and trees that had been there before history. Sophie looked at them and breathed. Help, her eyes said to the hills. Help, to the clouds, treetops, and grass. They bore her appeal like so many gods, with silence, no change of expression. She continued to look at them.

She continued to look at them, but addressed no more petitions. Words trivialised. Thought trivialised. Her unhappiness was so extraordinary that it was literally not to be thought of.

She stood motionless. But from a distance she was being stared at. After a time, her eyes were pulled to the cat's eyes, and she slowly roused herself and looked into them with some sense of obligation. Knowing it would come to her, Sophie drew a breath to summon the cat. Then she frowned and closed her mouth, repelled by her power over something more vulnerable than herself. She felt physically a nausea of the heart, and understood that 'heartsick' wasn't, after all, poetic rhetoric, but a description of a state of being. One which it would be preferable never to know.

Animals should beware of humans. How tempting, evidently, to play God and play games with little puppets for the sake of testing your skills…Sophie shivered and shook her head. Some humans should beware of others. All should learn early the safety limits of love and trust. But what a pity! How could you? How could you? she thought. And how could I? Some other day, if there was another day, she would think about these rights and wrongs.

Glancing again at the cat, who was still awaiting command, Sophie said, 'Be independent,' and feeling itself without instruction the cat prowled in a circle, curled up, and slept.

Caroline had stolen a remarkable pink rock from a faraway beach, a golden-pink rock worn into a chaise longue by the Pacific. Now Sophie lay on its sea-washed curves, supported and warmed, grateful to the rock. She closed her eyes and a single line creased her forehead. Minutes passed, and she opened her eyes. In the whole sky there were only three small clouds, three of Dalí's small, premonitory clouds, looking as unreal as his. It was possible that this time tomorrow, this time tomorrow, she would be dead.

Of whom, Sophie debated with herself coldly, might that not be said?

She made no response. It was unanswerably true that she had placed herself in the hands of death; she was in the airy halls of death now, with all formalities complete except the last one. Everywhere there was the certainty, the expectation, that she would make the final move at any moment. And it was so clear that the alternative to death was something worse.

If she lived, sooner or later this sorrow would go, and then she would change and be a different person and a worse one, dead in truth. For the sorrow was all that was left of the best she had had it in her to be, the best she had been able to offer the world, the result of the experiment that she was. So it was bound to seem of some importance, just now, while she could still understand it.

She gave a shallow sigh and shifted her position on the rock. In its frame of leaves the cat dozed. Everything altered minutely. The small painted clouds had disappeared. And, of course, it was foolish to complain. In a way, she had been quite surpassingly lucky; and there was a great deal left. The only thing that seemed to have vanished entirely, now that she had time to search among the ruins, was hope.

'Hope…' she said aloud, in a toneless voice. 'It's amazing what a difference it makes.'

The two women sat drinking coffee and glancing at their watches in the minutes to spare before leaving for the station and the Sydney train. For the twentieth time without success, Sophie sought to thank Caroline. 'Rubbish! I'm only sorry you're going so soon.' And they both smiled and rose from their chairs, glancing about to verify that Sophie's luggage was where she had placed it ten minutes earlier.

'Say goodbye to Cat,' Caroline ordered. 'You've made a friend there!' She swooped down on her pet and juggled it into Sophie's arms, before hurrying off to bring the car round to the front door.

For seconds Sophie held it against her chest, saying nothing whatever, feeling comforted by the weight, the warmth, the dumb communion, by the something like forbearance towards her of Caroline's cat. She let it leap down from the nest of her arms.

Lifting her bag, Sophie cast a final look at the silent room and its furnishings, and went to the door. As she turned the handle, with nothing in her mind but cars and trains and Caroline and, just beyond them all, the city looming, it occurred to her that, regardless of what was past, or what she now knew, she herself might still have the capacity to love. Need not, under some immutable compulsion, merely react. The idea presented itself in so many words. A telegram.

Like a soldier who, perhaps mortally wounded and lying in blood, hears a distant voice that means either death or survival, and unable to care, still half-lifts his head, Sophie listened.

Love…That poor debased word. Poor love. Oh, poor love, she thought. It was the core and essence of her nature, and a force in her compared with which any other was slight indeed. Still alive? Even yet? Ever again? More illusions? Good feeling? The psychic knives had finished all that. Surely? It only remained for her to follow. Surely?

Yet in the car, while she and Caroline exchanged remarks, Sophie's mind considered her chances. Now and then it condensed its findings and threw her a monosyllabic report, like a simple computer. Her changes were exactly that—a chance. And the sorrow...Only yesterday, the other day, she had believed that if she lived the sorrow would go and that she would then know a worse death than that of her body. But as it seemed *now* the sorrow would never go, could never leave her; like all else in life it had become an aspect of her person. As her love had. How strange, she thought, that nothing ever goes.

Nevertheless, detailing as they did the unconditional terms of her existence, these thoughts were in themselves a death. Had she been consulted, she would have chosen none of this, none of these steely thorns, inconceivable relinquishments. But no one had asked her; she had had no choice. One or two strengths and the love were what she had, and all she had, and what she would always have. And that was that.

Caroline said, 'Hear that clanking? I need a new car.'

Pedestrians cut through the tangle of traffic near the railway station. A dog pranced by looking for adventure. Sophie stared at shopping baskets, at boys on bikes, while debating the merits of this car over that with Caroline. 'Small ones are easier to park.'

Suicide produced just then, like a super-salesman, a picture of the very place. She knew it! Ideal, ideal. A hidden clearing off the track where you wouldn't be found too soon...

And the instruction resumed its endless cries of surprise, trying to save her. How could you, how could you, it said. The psychic knife went in, it said. The psychic blood came out.

Yes, yes, Sophie agreed. She had heard this many times before, and could only suppose the reiteration had once served a useful purpose. But how like a human organisation! Even at the place of instruction, the right hand did not know what the left was doing. Someone down the line had not yet been informed that times had changed; the long-expected message had been received and was under the deepest consideration.

Walking up the station ramp with Caroline, Sophie took no notice, letting the two sides battle it out. They would learn, they would learn. She had learned.

Acknowledgments

'The Fun of the Fair' was previously unpublished.

'Alice' was published in the *New Yorker*, 2015.

'The City at Night' was previously unpublished.

'Summertime' was published on *Literary Hub*, 2015.

'The North Sea' was published in *Canary Press*, 2015.

An abridged version of 'The Cornucopia' was published in *Harper's Magazine*, 2015.

'The Beautiful Climate' was published in *Kill Your Darlings*, 2015, and an earlier version was published in anthologies from the 1960s onwards.

An earlier version of 'Lance Harper, His Story' was published in *Australian Letters*, 1962, and in anthologies from the 1960s onwards.

An earlier version of 'The Cost of Things' was published in anthologies from the 1960s onwards.

An earlier version of 'English Lesson' was published in anthologies from the 1960s onwards.

'It Is Margaret' was published in *Australian Book Review*, 2015.

An earlier version of 'A Few Days in the Country' was published in *Overland*, 1977.

ALSO AVAILABLE FROM TEXT PUBLISHING
THE NOVELS OF ELIZABETH HARROWER

Down in the City
Introduced by Delia Falconer

The Catherine Wheel
Introduced by Ramona Koval

The Long Prospect
Introduced by Fiona McGregor

The Watch Tower
Introduced by Joan London

In Certain Circles